Into
Tordon

Into Tordon

Z.F. KINGBOLT

MidnightSun

First published 2016 by MidnightSun Publishing Pty Ltd
PO Box 3647, Rundle Mall, SA 5000, Australia.
www.midnightsunpublishing.com

Z.F. Kingbolt is a Northern Beaches Writers' Group pseudonym
Into Tordon is a collaborative project between:
  Editor-in-Chief: Zena Shapter
  Editors: Zoya Nojin • Zena Shapter
  Authors: Leah Boonthanom • Tracey Jackson • Liz Michell • Mijmark • Tony
  McFadden • Zoya Nojin • Kristin Prescott • Zena Shapter • Kirsten Taylor

www.zfkingbolt.com

Cataloguing-in-Publication entry is available from the
National Library of Australia.
http://catalogue.nla.gov.au

Cover design by Kim Lock and Jonathan Pearce

Printed and bound in Australia by Griffin Press. The papers used by
MidnightSun in the manufacture of this book are natural, recyclable products
made from wood grown in sustainable plantation forests.

For those who love games…

For those who love games...

Chapter 1

———

Beth studied the screen, her heart pounding. This was it—the level she'd fought to reach for months. A horde of angry beastmen raced towards her avatar, yelping as they leapt over the mossy rocks and logs of Tordon's forest. Spears were raised in their hands and saliva-dripping mutts bound beside them, barking and growling in frenzy. Beyond them, past towering tree columns, a hanging man swung from a gnarled old gumtree, his ropes creaking as he dangled over a square chasm. Beth's palms grew sweaty. Whoever cut down the hanging man would end the game and score fifty extra points, which would be enough to win Beth the entire championship. The *anniversary* championship.

As the thirty-second countdown began at the top of the screen, she wiped her hands on her jeans and tied her frizzy strawberry-coloured hair into a ponytail, just like her avatar. Some gamers were mean to girl-players in Tordon's chatroom, asking why they bothered gaming instead of hanging out at the mall. So Beth's avatar wasn't obviously a boy or girl. That way she could play in peace. Play and maybe one day…today…win?

Her father let out a loud snore from the lounge room. He'd stayed up late to stare at his favourite footy team losing on the television last night, and the whole house stank of popcorn and chips. Whatever. As long as he didn't move for another five minutes. With only three players left in the game, this level wouldn't last long.

To Beth's right was VlahPaul, his curly blond avatar readying his crossbow. She knew VlahPaul from school. His parents had a house on Marao Avenue with a view of the local tree farm and a big paperbark still standing in the backyard. Or so he said. He'd scored his crossbow in the game's sixth level and his point score placed him in third position.

To Beth's left, the player in second position, Zane007, faded into a crouched position, Jingum sword steadied. As usual, sleek black hair hid the face, but the avatar was obviously male. From watching Zane007 in previous games, Beth also knew he was the one to beat. Thankfully though, he had no lives left, and no shield, only the pentagonal Rune of Respect, which gave him greater energy. Looking at the approaching hordes, he would use the last of that here, and make sure it was to his advantage.

Still, Beth had the Cloak of Protection, which she'd won in the last level by activating the stone-bear Rune of Compassion. She had one life left too. And, as the emerald forest clearing filled with beastmen, it was *her* avatar in first place, pole position.

So she readied her Jingum sword and repeated Tordon's Kumdo philosophy in her mind—*discipline, concentration, endurance*. One day, she'd learn the martial art of Kumdo for real. But for now the only thing she wanted was her name at the top of The Chameleon Chart. Only those who lived within ten kilometres of 106 Daintree Street, where Tordon's developer Aaron Kaleski once lived, could compete in the monthly championship games, and there was no telling how long Dad would be able to afford their current house without a job. Next month, she might live too far away. Now was her chance. Imagine being the first girl to ever win too—and on the Chart's first anniversary! Everyone at school followed the Chart, so if she won she'd finally get to tell them that she, Bethlyn Gatise, was BGwarrior, and they'd stop saying, 'you're a loser like your dad'. She might even win some proper friends, ones who realised she was actually good at something.

The timer began flashing—ten seconds to go. This was it!

5—4—3

Tribes of beastmen roared, mutts barked and a bowl clanged to the floor in Beth's lounge room. She winced and quickly turned down the volume.

3—2—1

Game on.

A horn blared and the beasts sprang forward. Beth jumped into a triple somersault over the tall grass in front of her. She landed on a rock pile just as a mass of beastmen and their mutts swarmed around her. Beyond them, immense trees towered into the pale sky. The sound of slashing swords and flying arrows grew louder. Zane007 and VlahPaul were already busy. They'd get a point for every beast they killed. But Beth didn't care about single points anymore. She had to get to the chasm and to that hanging man.

So she sliced her sword at any beastman who leapt toward her rock while glancing at the trees. If she could get into their branches somehow, she could jump from trunk to trunk and miss most of the beasts, as well as the time-consuming slashing that came with them.

Except the edge of the clearing was too far away. A single somersault would land her right in the middle of battle.

Unless…that's right! She still had some rocks of her own to use.

She selected a rock from her backpack and threw it at a pack of beastmen about a somersault away.

Splat!

Five died instantly. Their black blood oozed out from under the rock like oil, even more when Beth somersaulted on top of it. Their mutts howled angrily. But two more rocks, ten more men, and she was within jumping distance of a tall grey tree. Its angular branches twisted into landing zones, but something gleamed lower down. A rune!

Shaped like a skull with three holes, it was the Rune of Self-Belief, granting extra strength as well as five extra points. But it hung so low Beth would have to jump down to reach it, where beasts would quickly surround her. So she leapt high into the tree, and left the rune for Zane007 or VlahPaul. Let it distract one of them.

Up in the branches, however, where wind muted the sound of battle, the chime of someone claiming the Rune of Death was loud enough. Someone would now get double points for any kill. She had no time to waste.

'Bethlyn?'

'Hang on a sec, Dad.'

He came into the room and hovered behind her chair. 'Somersault more to the left,' he whispered.

'I am!'

'Okay. Sorry.'

Beth cringed, wishing he'd stop apologising for everything, then zoned back into the game, trunk-jumping and branch-spinning until the hanging man was in sight. She'd saved a lot of time, but of course the old gumtree hanging off the chasm's edge was surrounded by a clearing full of beastmen. She had no choice now but to jump into combat and start swiping.

Dad leaned in and gripped the back of her chair. 'Now what, Bethie?'

'This,' she said, jumping. Slicing with the control of a 10th Dan Kumdo master, she struck left and right, behind and over her, slashing through the swarm to reach the bottom of the tree. Her Cloak of Protection faded, her avatar grunted with every stroke, but her point score raced up and she reached the tree alive, only to realise she should have given more thought to how she'd free the hanging man and less thought to her speed.

Yes, she was the first to reach the gnarled old gumtree.

But somewhere in the forest behind her was a petal stone—the Rune of Remedy. She had probably swung right over it. What a stupid decision! Now she faced climbing a tree that would kill her with just one touch, for its trunk was coated in steaming purple goo—poison.

Chapter 2

Touching any purple goo in Tordon meant losing a life. Beth had learnt that the hard way in the game's second level. She checked her stats.

'One life left,' said Dad.

'I know! I don't know where I'll re-spawn though—in the tree, mid-way up it, or back below?'

The sound of slashing came closer. Another player was nearby. She glanced at her stats and noticed the apple symbol alongside her satchel. That's right, she still had the apple-tree seed she'd found in level one. Selecting the seed, she planted it firmly in the ground beside the old gumtree.

Whoosh!

Tiny green shoots sprouted and grew to maturity within seconds.

'Go, Bethie, go!' said Dad, spurring her on with a glimmer of something in his voice she hadn't heard in a while.

She grit her teeth and leapt into the tree's expanding branches as it shot up alongside the gumtree. She would win this for both of them. It grew past the heights of any poison and into the empty air over the chasm. The hanging man's swinging rope squeaked like the slow tick of a clock.

Dad patted her back and Beth grinned. She was close.

She found the apple tree's tallest branch and climbed up, crawling along it as far as she could without it snapping, then stretched out her sword.

It wasn't close enough to cut the rope!

A gulf of air separated her, the rope and the figure swinging below. A glint of gold shone somewhere on the chasm floor. What was that? A golden rune? A house?

A branch snapped on the apple tree below her—Zane007 was climbing up behind her. She had to do something! Could she jump onto the old gumtree from here? No, there were no angled branches designed for players to land. Still, jumping would let her reach the rope, possibly cut it. She had a life left too. Even if she died trying, she might still win. With Zane007 almost there, it was worth a try.

She somersaulted high into the air and sailed down towards the rope with her sword reaching. With a swish, she sliced the hanging man free, then fell to her death at the base of the chasm. There was a chime as her last life extinguished.

But…she re-spawned, as the winner!

'You did it!' crowed Dad as if his footy team had finally won.

'I can't believe it.'

Fanfares and cheers heralded the end of the championship. Beth's point score rocketed by fifty points. Fireworks exploded over her character, which was now standing on the chasm floor. Her character's name, BGwarrior, flashed across the screen—beside it the word 'winner'. Beth held her breath as her character automatically strolled towards the golden glint she'd seen from the apple tree, and had only hoped would be the Chameleon's house. Whether the championship was held in an ice fortress, a desert or a forest, Tordon's gamemaster, the Chameleon, welcomed every winner into the Golden House of Fame. And this time, it was her!

The famous Black-Door-With-No-Doorknob slid upwards to reveal a tall moustached figure with bright green eyes and a cape—the Chameleon. A red snake hung around his neck and its tongue flicked out as the Chameleon bowed. Above the doorway was an address: 106 Daintree Street.

Beth peered at the screen. That address had never been above the doorway before. But then, she'd never won before.

The Chameleon winked and gestured for her character to pass inside. As soon as she did the black door fell behind them, leaving her name and the word 'winner' flashing onscreen. The address had vanished and in its place were the words: *Only champions dare to enter.*

'This calls for a fizzy drink,' said Dad, ruffling her hair and heading into the kitchen.

Beth turned to watch him go. Was that happiness in his voice? Could this be a sign of things to come, a return to normal?

Beth smiled and leaned back in her chair, mesmerised by her flashing name as if it had the power to grant new beginnings. Dad had seemed proud of her. And she bet no one would call her a loser now at school. She'd won The Chameleon Chart on its first anniversary! After all the daily games, weekly tournaments and monthly championships, she was finally the best of them all!

She leant forward and navigated through the dropdown menus to find the complete results. They were already listed under 'The Chameleon Chart' tab.

User	Point Score
BGwarrior	3252
Zane007	3203
VlahPaul	2998
6thDan	2596
AxaMax	2143
Sam2014	1989
|8-<	1950
DeathStar	1822
TaoMaster	1715
Wolk	1704

Beth stared at the screen. Where was DaveT? He'd won last month's championship, but now he wasn't even in the top ten? The best players tended to compete month after month. Still, the most important name to note was hers—there at the top. She had won. Now, and for the next whole month, hers would be the first name every Tordon gamer would see when they clicked on The Chameleon Chart.

Wait, no—not just when they clicked on the chart.

Beth navigated back to the home page and searched the side menu. Yes! There was her name. For the next whole *year* they'd see who'd won the anniversary championship, Tordon's hardest challenge yet. She grinned. Now everyone would know she'd won.

They would know, wouldn't they?

She pulled a strand of hair over her shoulder and began to chew on it. What if nobody figured it out? Her character had her colouring, but it also looked like a boy, as she'd intended.

'Bethlyn!' her father called from the kitchen.

'Yeah?'

'Isn't the food supposed to come between twelve and one o'clock?'

'What's the time on the microwave?'

'Oh, right. Sorry.'

Beth swallowed. His voice had returned to that same grey droop she heard every day. Didn't he remember she'd won? Everything was going to be different now.

A flicker to the right of the screen caught her attention. It showed the latest comments from the chatroom:

6thDan—You were cheated Zane007! That move shouldn't have been allowed.

Zane007—Thanks for your support 6thDan. But if it weren't allowed, BGwarrior wouldn't have been able to do it.

6thDan—I'd like to see how leaping off a cliff would work for a Kumdo master in real life!

Blood rushed to Beth's cheeks as she clicked through to the chatroom. Under the name of each user was their avatar. 6thDan had chosen the traditional wire-grilled Kumdo helmet rather than show his face. Zane007's avatar showed tanned skin and blue eyes under his floppy black hair. She'd chatted with him online many times before, which is probably why he was defending her now. It was nice of him, especially since he'd only just missed out on winning. She typed her reply.

BGwarrior—Thanks Zane007. You played a great game. I had no idea jumping would work. But I had to do something—you were right behind me!

She chewed on her hair while waiting for a reply. Finally the next comment loaded.

Zane007—Your risk paid off.

Beth smiled. She knew he'd be gracious; he always was. She wondered if he really looked like his avatar in real life. Tanned skin was pretty unusual given the sun restrictions at school. She had no idea if he went to her school or not, but he must live somewhere locally because of the ten kilometre rule. The chatroom updated.

VlahPaul—I agree with 6thDan. This is a game of skill and sportsmanship. A player should not ever win by dying BGwarrior! A real Kumdo wouldn't!

What a ridiculous thing to say! The loophole was there, so she'd used it. They should all be congratulating her! As for real life, most people couldn't do triple somersaults either, but that didn't stop any of them somersaulting in the game. What was the matter with them all?

BGwarrior—It's a game remember! No one here is a real Kumdo master.
6thDan—Speak for yourself BGwarrior. Unlike many who play this game, I am a real student of Kumdo.
BGwarrior—So your avatar is true? You have a helmet and Kumdo sword and everything?
6thDan—I do. Along with my brown belt.

A brown belt? Is that why he was so mean about her win? And VlahPaul too? They were clearly jealous. 6thDan probably wasn't even a Kumdo student.

BGwarrior—A brown belt? Really?
6thDan—Meet me outside the mall during this arvo's let-out and I'll show you.
VlahPaul—I'd like to see a real Kumdo sword. If you have one 6thDan...?

Zane007—Me too. 4pm?
6thDan—It would be great to meet you true champions. Bring a candle.

True champions? Beth ground her teeth together. This was not how she'd imagined winning. And why were they suggesting the mall? Did they suspect she was a girl, is that why they were being so mean?

She remembered the message over the famous Black-Door-With-No-Doorknob. *Only champions dare to enter.* It gave her an idea.

BGwarrior—The mall sucks. Let's meet somewhere way cooler—106 Daintree Street.
6thDan—What, so Kaleski's ghost can explain how cheaters win? Sounds good.
VlahPaul—Ha! I'll be there.
Zane007—Me too.

Beth slammed her finger on the word 'logout'. Cheater? It was a strategy game! 6thDan probably didn't even have a real sword. Who'd be the cheater then? And why bring a candle?

The gate bell rang.

'Can you get it?' her father called. He was back in front of the TV, with two glasses and the fizzy drink bottle resting beside him. He hadn't even poured it.

With a sigh, Beth rose and went to the front door, wincing at their shabby furniture and worn carpet, even if it was only the delivery man. She buzzed the driveway gate open and it rattled across with age and rust. The smell of roast chicken wafted into the house and her stomach grumbled. Although she had to unpack the shopping, at least lunch would be quick and she'd have plenty of time to meet the Tordon players she'd beaten earlier.

That's right—*beaten*.

No matter what they thought, she'd won, and it would be exciting to meet other gamers as a winner. Surely not everyone would think like 6thDan. Zane007 had already stuck up for her. She'd have plenty of fans on her side. Some of them might even turn out to be the friends she'd been waiting to win over.

On the other hand, how were they going to react when they met the anniversary champion, already labelled a cheat by some, and it was *her*?

Chapter 3

Beth pulled down her sleeves as she hurried to Daintree Street. Behind tall fences, in tree-less backyards, little voices filled the air along with the floral scent of government-issued sunscreen. Children were allowed to play outside during the afternoon let-out, but only younger kids generally did. Most kids Beth's age were on their devices this time of day, playing in some virtual space. Beth yanked down her sleeves some more. The sun was really pressing down today. Most kids her age also got new tops every growth-spurt, but Dad had been out of work so long now... He'd once been a manager at the tree-farm, but since he'd lost his job, everything had changed. He'd changed. Mum had died when Beth was four, still he'd kept his job—his parenting responsibilities keeping him focussed. Now with this latest set-back he was falling apart. Was it because she was old enough now to take care of herself?

Beth straightened her back. He'd get another job soon, she was sure.

Well, he would if he stopped moping around watching the dumb footy.

Someone sneezed behind a fence, making Beth jump. The permanent haze of dust and pollution that hung over her suburb often worsened people's allergies. At least Beth had zero allergies—not to pollen, dust mites, pets, mosquitoes, wheat, nuts, dairy, food colouring, egg, fish, soya *or* mould. These days, her teachers said, she was a rarity.

Ten minutes later she hurried into Daintree Street—a quiet road with fewer houses, where the fences were lower and wild grass crept through. Sweat broke on her brow from the sun. When she was younger, quiet streets like this one would have been lined with trees offering shade. They were all gone now, even from this older area, chopped down by thieves when the Tree Protection Laws made raw wood valuable enough to be stolen.

Beth spied a group of teens gathered around someone wearing a complete Kumdo outfit—billowing blue pants and a heavy blue jacket bound by a brown belt. Above his head the boy brandished a long thin Juk-To practice sword. She read the back of his jacket—Lee Sang Hwan Academy. It had to be 6thDan.

Reaching the group, she glanced around. There were so many people here. Some wore allergy-masks and it seemed everyone could afford long sleeves. Her stomach clenched. Where was Zane007?

'I knew it wouldn't be a real sword,' someone behind her said.

She turned to see a tall boy with curly blond hair and a mass of freckles covering his face. VlahPaul. Behind him was another tall boy—olive-skinned with dark hair and blue eyes. It had to be Zane007! His clothes were stylish too, just like his avatar, though he was a bit pudgier in real life.

'Zane007?'

'Yeah, that's me.' He glanced at her. 'But it's just Zane.'

Beth coloured. Of course. How stupid of her.

'Hi Pauly!' cooed a girl with perfectly smooth long brown hair. She raced over, linked her arm through VlahPaul's and planted a kiss on his cheek.

'Hi Wolk.' VlahPaul grinned, winking at Zane.

Beth smiled even as Zane scowled. Now she would meet *four* players from this month's championship. 'It's nice to meet you, Wolk.'

The girl ignored her. 'Check out the cool sword, Pauly.'

'It's not a proper sword,' Zane growled. He flicked his hair and the crowd parted. 'I thought you were bringing real steel.' He glanced around, but Beth noticed his gaze rested on Wolk. 'You can't fight with that.'

VlahPaul snorted. 'Reckon you could show him, 007? You just *love* all that fighting stuff.'

'Oh yes,' sneered Wolk. 'Your army dad must've shown you *loads*.' And she threw such a venomous look at Zane that Beth drew back.

'Sure. I know a few moves.' Zane clenched his jaw before striding forward. He towered over most of the group. 6thDan smiled and started to bow in greeting, but paused when Zane reached out and twanged the yellow string stretching along the sword's plastic spine. 'Except this is a cheap kid's toy.'

'It's a modern competition sword,' said 6thDan, turning red. 'I have a steel Jukkum at home, but Father said I'd be arrested if I brought it onto the street.'

Fair enough, thought Beth.

'Sounds like dog's buns,' Zane said to 6thDane, making some of the others chuckle. 'Is that what you are too—dog's buns?'

More laughter.

6thDan lowered his eyes.

Beth stepped forward. 'You said to bring a candle?' She offered him a long white candle she'd found under the kitchen sink.

6thDan glanced up at her. 'Thanks.' He nodded to a few other candles on the pavement, bound in an elastic band.

'I have a match,' said VlahPaul to murmurs of surprise.

'A match! Is it made of wood?'

'How did you get one of those?' asked Zane.

'I have my sources,' said VlahPaul smugly.

'Could you light the candles then?' asked 6thDan.

'No,' he replied. 'I just brought it to show you.'

6thDan rolled his eyes and passed a lighter to Beth. 'Could you please light them while I get ready?'

'Isn't there a fire ban?' said Zane and he glared at Beth like she was dog's buns too.

She looked away. 'Not at the moment.' She crouched to add her candle to the stack, then lit all the wicks.

When enough wax had melted, she dripped it onto the pavement and pushed the upright stack into it. The wax cooled, held the candles steady, and their flames united in a smoky yellow column. Satisfied, Beth stepped back, and realised everyone had been watching. Did they recognise her yet?

No, their eyes were fixed on the candles, expectation in their faces. Beth had a sense that even the dark windows of the old houses around them watched. Wait, weren't they supposed to be outside Kaleski's house? Her gaze scanned the street. Which house was his?

A groan erupted beside her and she turned to see 6thDan gripping his weapon as if wringing out a towel. He moved forward and wafted the sword over the flames. The movement didn't even make the smoke stir. Slowly he raised it above his head and took a deep breath.

'Kum Ki,' he explained, 'is achieved by joining internal and external energy into oneness. To do it, you have to master Danjun, breathing as well as absorbing the earth's energy through your hands. Ki moves around, over and in the body, and then,' he yanked the sword through the air like an explosion, stopping just before the candle's flame. It went out instantly.

Beth gasped along with the crowd.

'Everyone has inner energy,' he looked around at the amazed faces. 'They just don't know how to release it.'

'Looks like a cheap trick to me,' Zane scoffed.

'Could you do that?' Beth asked him.

Zane peered at her face. 'Do I know you?'

'I'm Beth, Bethlyn Gatise.'

'And that's supposed to mean something to me?'

'My initials are BG. I'm BGwarrior. Remember I said I'd meet you guys here?'

Zane snickered and shook his head as if enjoying a private joke.

VlahPaul stepped closer, looking her up and down. '*You're* the champion of The Chameleon Chart's first anniversary game?'

Beth smiled. He was the first person to say it aloud.

'Hey, aren't you from my school?' someone called from the back of the crowd. 'The one whose dad got fired from the tree-farm?'

Beth's chest tightened. 'He quit!'

'That's not what I heard—what a loser!'

'Yeah, *loser*!'

'Come on, Pauly.' Wolk wrinkled her nose at Beth. 'There're too many fakes around here.'

A murmur of agreement spread through the crowd and some began drifting away.

Beth watched in disbelief. 'I *am* the Champion!'

VlahPaul just looked at her in disgust. 'As if.'

Beth searched the faces of the others. How could she prove it to them? Her eyes stopped on 6thDan still swishing his sword. 'Can I have a go of your Juk-To?'

He shook his head, not even looking her in the eye. 'You have no respect. Your courage has no courtesy.'

'What do you mean?'

'He means,' said Zane, grabbing 6thDan's sword, 'that no true champion would jump off a cliff to win. Dying in the heat of battle is fine. But to win like you did is cowardly.'

The blood rushed to Beth's face. 'But that's not what you said in the chatroom.'

Zane rolled his eyes. 'Only idiots say what they really think online.' He swished the sword around his body.

'Okay, give it back now,' said 6thDan, trying to snatch the sword.

'Go 007!' said VlahPaul with a laugh.

Beth stepped forward, sick of them all. There were no friends to be made here. 'Give it back, Zane.'

'Why, you gonna win it back by throwing yourself off a cliff?'

'You know,' said Beth, clenching her fists, 'it's called strategy. Sometimes you have to make sacrifices to win. The championship might be configured that way for all we know.'

Zane pointed the sword at the house opposite them. 'Go on then.'

'Go on what?'

'Go ask.'

VlahPaul gave a bark of laughter.

Beth stared across the road. So that's where the famous Tordon developer once lived. Behind the low fence was a two-storey house, its lower windows sealed up with bricks and its yellow paint old and peeling. Weeds grew waist-high in the garden. A shadow flickered in the attic window and she shuddered, remembering hearing stories that only ghosts lived there now.

'No one lives there anymore,' she said quietly.

'You sure about that?' asked Zane, raising his eyebrows at the window.

'I heard he moved to India,' said 6thDan, finally grabbing back his sword. 'Keeps this place ready so he can come back to it one day.'

'India?'

'Yeah, to Ripple headquarters. You know they're the best in gaming now.'

'*I* heard,' said Wolk, sliding alongside Zane, 'that Ripple fired him.'

'No,' Zane snapped. 'They made him redundant.'

'Same thing,' said 6thDan.

'No it isn't,' Zane said.

'What's your problem, Zane?'

'You.' Zane glared down at 6thDan. 'Wasting my time with this toy.'

6thDan tensed and thrust out his sword. 'Come on then.'

'*I* heard,' said Beth to break the tension, 'that Kaleski discovered a gateway to another dimension.'

'I heard that too,' said Wolk, gazing toward the house. 'It's where he got his inspiration for Tordon. It's based on somewhere real.'

Zane rolled his eyes again. 'That's just dumb.'

Wolk glared at him.

'Either way, 007,' VlahPaul smiled, 'you should probably escort the *champion* over for a closer look, given she's a girl and all.'

Wolk's grin was triumphant. 'Yes! Surely by *now* your

father's taught you how to protect a lady.'

Zane scowled at Wolk and VlahPaul. They stared back. 'Of course!' he suddenly said, tossing his head at Beth. 'Coming?'

Beth glanced at 6thDan, who still looked ready to chop Zane with his sword, then she looked back at the house. She was curious, plus there'd been that strange message at the end of the game. *Only champions dare to enter.*

She nodded. 'I *am* the champion.' She stepped onto the road and Zane followed.

When they reached the house's low fence Beth hesitated, but Zane just slipped around its rotting gate and strode up the driveway.

'Only champions dare to enter,' she mumbled to herself before hurrying after him.

'You're trespassing!' 6thDan called after them. 'It's against the law, you know.'

Wolk and VlahPaul said nothing, just crossed the road and waited by the gate.

'Keep walking,' Zane said, glancing at the upstairs window.

Beth nodded and squinted at a small rusted plaque set on the house's front wall. *Video Surveillance In Use.* So was this place occupied or not? No sounds came from its grounds. No lights shone from inside. It certainly looked abandoned.

'Don't you think it looks a lot like the house in the game?' asked Zane.

Beth frowned and took a sideways step. 'Yeah, maybe from this angle.' The driveway led them around the side of the house to where its front door sat between two sealed windows. Upstairs were two more windows, lined up with those below. 'And look at the door.'

The door was black and gleamed as if made of metal. It had no doorknob, handle or knocker—nothing to open it by, just like Tordon's famous Black-Door-With-No-Doorknob.

'That's strange though.' Beth pointed to a shiny silver keypad in the wall beside the door, its tiny buttons lit and glowing.

'Yeah,' said Zane, 'because if the house is abandoned, why is the electricity still on?'

'Security?' Beth shrugged.

'Come on, guys!' 6thDan called again. 'I'm leaving!'

'This is boring,' Wolk whined. 'Let's go Pauly.'

'Not yet,' said VlahPaul, 'I'm waiting to see what our winners will do. Maybe they'll go in.'

Zane folded his arms. '*She's* the winner! If anyone's going in, it's her!'

Beth ignored them all, her attention caught by the keypad. She leaned closer. 'Whoa—check it out.'

'What?' Zane peered over her shoulder.

'Oh, I get it,' her eyes widened. Each keypad button was engraved with a number and a symbol, each of which resembled Tordon runes. There was the skull Rune of Self-Belief, a four-rods Rune of Death, the pentagonal Rune of Respect, the stone-bear Rune of Compassion, a petal Rune of Remedy...

Zane started pressing buttons. He tried the number of

the house followed by its postcode. Next he tried Beth's final point score.

'I think the symbols have something to do with it.' Beth gestured at the engravings. 'Which level did you get that Rune of Respect in, seven? What rune was in level one?'

'The Rune of Survival,' he said, pointing to the symbol of a ceramic jug.

'What about the second level?'

'I think I get it,' he interrupted.

VlahPaul called out then. 'You're right, Wolk, this is boring! Why on earth are we hanging out with these *losers?*'

Wolk burst into laughter and they walked off, the rest of the group drifting away with them. As their voices faded into the distance, Zane tapped each keypad symbol in the order their respective runes had appeared in the game. 'You'll see!' he muttered as if Beth couldn't hear. 'I'll show you who's a loser.' He pressed the last rune won in the game—the Rune of Death—and with a click and a whoosh, the door flew up into the ceiling, disappearing into a slot in the door frame.

'No way,' said Beth.

Beyond the doorway was a hall of dark floorboards and a shadowy wooden staircase. On the walls was a floral wallpaper, covered in a thin coat of white paint and peeling away in places.

'Time to claim your winner's prize, BGwarrior!' Zane grabbed Beth's arm.

'Hey, get off!'

But Zane pushed Beth towards a huge cobweb that hung across the entrance. Beth pushed back, but Zane was too strong, his grip on her arm secure.

'Stop it!'

'What? Not gonna risk your life to win this one?'

Beth remembered the Chameleon's message: *Only champions dare to enter.*

'Actually, I do dare.' She took a big step forward.

With no resistance to his pushing, Zane tripped on the doorstep and tumbled into the cobweb himself.

Beth laughed, then realised Zane's was still gripping her arm. He pulled her down with him and she tumbled into the cobweb too. As her knees slammed onto the hall floorboards, the sticky web coated her face, hands and arms. Something flashed.

'Yuck! It's everywhere!' Zane cried.

'Ew!' Beth cried, blinking and frantically plucking at her lips, eyelids and hair. It stuck like glue!

Then a gust of wind blew over her body. A sliding noise sounded behind her, followed by a loud slam.

'What the...?' Zane said, sounding panicked somewhere nearby.

Beth blinked as the tacky web cleared from her face. The floorboards beneath her were covered in brittle leaves that crunched as she sat back on her heels. She tried brushing the web from her hands but it wouldn't come off, and the more she pulled at it the thicker it stuck, gripping her hands like the thin rubber gloves doctors used. Her plucking made its surface less sticky, but still the tough mesh remained.

'What's happening?' cried Zane.

Beth looked up, expecting to see the hallway staircase. Instead, trees towered around them and through a leafy canopy she could see blue sky. Her mouth gaped. Trees! So many of them, and not caged in a tree farm! Where was the house, the floorboards and staircase? The scent of smoke wafted towards her on the warm breeze. Birds called, insects buzzed, and in the distance was a low rumble that sounded like…men roaring?

She snatched up the nearest leaf, crumpled and smelled it. It was mint, like her chewing gum.

Were they in a real forest?

Or was she dreaming?

No, her arm was sore from where Zane had gripped it—this wasn't a dream. But what had happened, where were they? Rumours had long floated around the Tordon chatroom that Kaleski had discovered a gateway to another dimension or world. Was this it?

'Just gotta get this door, argh, come *on*!' Zane shouted.

Beth turned. The trunk of a massive tree—the kind she only saw in history books of once great rainforests—now crowded the space where they'd entered the house. Zane was trying to get a grip on the outline of a front door, but it was slowly fading, its edges blending into the bark.

Beth jumped up, her eyes wide. There had to be another door.

She spun around searching each trunk and the spaces

between. But there was none. How were they going to get home?

Zane yelled and thumped the wood of the large tree, but the door had already disappeared. In its place was an inscription, etched deep into the bark: *Once a killing, twice the killing*.

What did that mean? There were two of them, but what about the killing part? She just wanted to go home now.

Home. Beth felt anger grow inside her. They were in the middle of a strange nowhere, with no obvious way of getting back, and it was all *his* fault—Zane, Mr 007 tough-guy. Her fists clenched and she felt a tightening on her hands. The webbing was still stuck there. Had it thickened? A network of solid white lines crisscrossed her palms and around each finger. At each wrist was a thick white band with a glowing circle divided into segments. She tried pulling it off again, but tugging just pinched her skin. It was like rubber had melted onto her flesh.

'What *is* this?' Zane was also tugging at whatever coated his hands.

'I have no idea,' Beth snapped. 'But you'd better figure it out, fast!'

'Why me? You're the champion.'

'Because you got us into this mess. So you can get us out!'

Zane turned on her then, fuming. 'Me? You tricked me, trapped me inside this place! What did you do?'

'*You* pushed *me*, remember!' she shouted as if 6thDan's

inner Ki energy would flow through her voice and smack him down.

Zane's reply was stopped by a horrid shriek from the treetops above them. He stared up. 'What was that?'

'I don't know,' said Beth, searching the tall forest again for any resemblance to the hallway from before. In the distance, she thought she saw something with a spear racing towards her. But that couldn't be right.

None of this was right.

Another shriek.

'What do we do?' moaned Zane, parting leaves on the ground as if hoping to find a weapon. 'What do we do?'

'I don't know.' Beth jumped as a branch cracked above them. 'But I think something's coming!'

They gazed up into the thick vines dangling from the highest branches. What stared back was a multi-eyed monstrosity with fur, tentacles, sharp claws and huge fangs. It swung towards them, using vines to move through the trees like a giant hairy octopus. With every swing it glared harder as if incensed with a ravenous hunger.

Beth changed her mind—she knew exactly what to do.

'Run!'

Chapter 4

Beth spun around and sprinted as the monstrous creature shrieked again, and again—louder and louder as it followed them through the greenery, swinging from vine to vine. Low ferns smacked into her as she ran over the uneven forest floor. She swatted them aside while hopping over stones, buttress roots and tangles of undergrowth. She didn't notice the spines on the branch in front of her until it was too late.

'Ow!' she yelled as it tore into her top and dug into her right arm. Blood oozed and it stung. Beth pressed her lips together and pushed on through the trees—she was not going to die here! Dad didn't even know where she'd gone!

'Slow—down!' Zane panted, falling behind.

But they couldn't slow down—the thing was right behind them! 'Come on! You'll get us both killed!' She grabbed his arm and pulled him with her. He may be to blame for their being here, but she wasn't going to struggle through it alone!

She noticed a brightness to their right.

'A clearing!' she shouted, pointing. 'No vines! It might not be able to move without vines or branches.' She glanced behind them. The thing was gaining on them, using its horrible tentacles to swing ever closer. She yanked Zane to the right and the brightness grew. Almost there! It looked to be a vast field.

Was that voices? It sounded like there was a large crowd up ahead.

Beth sped up, but as soon as they broke through the undergrowth, she wished they hadn't—the voices didn't belong to people, but a group of strange beast-like tribesmen charging forward, some with horns, others with fur, hooves, tails and claws. Most wore the familiar animal skins and tribal ornaments of...Tordon? Saliva-dripping mutts raced by their sides. All of them held raised spears, and one of them angled his weapon as if to throw it. He lunged and its tip glinted in the sun as it shot towards them.

'Duck!' she screamed, spinning ninety degrees and dragging Zane along the tree edge.

Spears whizzed through the air.

There was a colossal thud and a shriek as the tentacled beast fell to the ground.

'Keep running!' she yelled. 'I don't think they've seen us!'

'I need—to rest,' panted Zane as they neared the far edge of the field.

Beth glanced back. The tribesmen were busy with the tentacled monster-thing, crowding around it and jumping up and down in celebration. Zane's breath was ragged and he was running bent over, clutching at his side. She switched to a fast walk and let go of Zane's arm. 'We can rest over there.' She pointed to where the field sloped down towards forest again, though the trees there seemed clear of vines.

'I smell smoke,' said Zane.

Beth looked but couldn't see what he meant. There was a dirt track, though, leading between the trees at the bottom of the slope.

'Grrr,' something snarled behind them. A mutt crept towards them from the trees on their right, saliva drooling from its muzzle. It crouched low, ready to pounce.

'Quick!' Beth yelled, turning and sprinting towards the track. Bursting onto what looked like a pathway, she stumbled on the roots of a tall tree.

'Move!' Zane shouted, slamming her aside.

She glanced back but the mutt wasn't following. 'Where is it?'

'I threw it a stick!'

'And?' she called after him, but if he replied she didn't hear him over the roar of tribesmen. Whatever Zane had done must have caught their attention, because now the whole tribe were racing towards them. Beth took off after Zane, following the path until they ran into a cleared area that seemed to be a camp. She gasped. Several log seats circled a smouldering fire neatly contained by rocks. They were burning wood? So precious back home, yet here it was being destroyed.

She looked around. A number of hammocks were slung high in the trees, covered by palm leaf shelters.

Pots and pans were stacked to one side of the fire, and its smoke curled upwards in a breeze tinged with mint and sweet basil. Zane was already across the space at what looked like a pile of weapons, picking up something long and thin.

'Hey, what are you doing? That's not yours!'

'Suit yourself,' he said, 'but I'm having this.' He held up a spear with four shiny points at one end. 'And this sword too.' It wasn't anything as elegant as a Kumdo sword, but it was sharp and metal. It was also, therefore, a good idea.

Beth hurried to the stack of weapons. The swords had crudely-shaped blades and were heavier than they looked. While Zane slashed his around to test its balance, Beth could barely lift hers. Maybe there was a lighter one? Yes, there at the back—a long thin blade with a lightweight handle. She had to move several aside to reach it, but it was the perfect weight.

Just in time.

The mutt was creeping up on them.

It bounded into the camp and leapt at her, its teeth bared and its claws stretched and sharp. Beth froze, but Zane didn't hesitate. He dashed forward, swinging his spear into the mutt's side.

'The beastmen of Tordon!' Zane cried, and it fell to the ground with a high-pitched whine.

Beth grimaced, but Zane picked up another spear and aimed it at the trees, ready.

'Athul!' came a voice. 'Athul, Athul?'

A group of roaring tribesmen charged into the camp.

Beth pointed her sword, gripping it with both hands.

But the tribesmen slowed on spying their dead mutt and lowered their spears completely.

Zane, however, was throwing his. 'Take that!' he shouted, laughing as the spear embedded itself deep into the arm of a tribesman. 'Score!'

The tribesman screamed in agony and grasped his furry arm, now dripping with blood. Bright—red—blood. Just like theirs.

'Fifty extra points to me!' Zane yelled.

The injured tribesman's friends surrounded him. Wherever Kaleski's Black-Door-With-No-Doorknob had transported them, these seemed to be real creatures, with a home, relationships and pets.

Zane pulled his arm back, preparing to throw another spear.

'Stop!' Beth cried. 'They're not attacking!'

Zane paused and his wild look faded as one of the tribesmen dropped to the ground, whimpering beside the mutt.

'Athul,' he murmured, his eyes full of despair.

'What have you done?' said Beth.

The rest of the tribesmen eyed them angrily and shook their spears.

'Oops.' Zane took a step back and glanced about. Then he suddenly turned and ran into the forest.

'Wait!' Beth yelled, plunging into the undergrowth after him.

He wouldn't slow.

'Zane! Wait!'

The tribesmen didn't seem to be following them—their voices faded the further Beth and Zane ran. Still Zane didn't stop—not until the forest floor began to incline up a ridge. Then he changed his pace to a fast walk. 'But we're in Tordon,' he was muttering to himself when Beth caught up to him, 'once the killing, twice the killing—I don't understand.' He looked up. 'Let's get up this hill, then we'll have a vantage point to see where we are.'

Beth gazed up the looming hill. She'd never hiked before. Ha! She'd never fallen through a dimensional gateway before either—who knew what was a good idea here and what wasn't? Tears pressed behind her eyes as she trudged after Zane. This wasn't supposed to be happening. She'd just wanted to meet some other gamers. Now all she wanted was to go home. Perhaps from higher up they'd be able to see a way?

Swallowing hard, she pushed up the hill. Crying wasn't going to get her home.

The further up the hill they hiked, the thicker the vegetation grew and they had to slash at it with their swords. Everything was so *green*! The path grew wetter and muddier and steeper. Shadows lengthened and Beth noticed vines growing here and there. They tramped on regardless, silent with their thoughts, even when spiked ferns scratched their skin and clothes. Bugs swarmed around their sweating faces and Beth jumped with each bird cry from the trees overhead—feeling as if something was going to attack them any moment. Zane kept grumbling so she knew it bothered him too.

They came across a small dell covered in mossy stones and fallen tree trunks. Several boulders sat to one side, clumped together under a vertical rockface that towered behind them. Water dripped down the sides of the boulders into a small clear puddle that glistened in the dim light. Beth slumped beside it and Zane threw his sword on the ground before falling to his knees, breathing hard. He eyed the liquid as if it were priceless. His sweat-soaked hair looked ridiculous now, draping over his brow like a freshly wrung mop.

He rinsed his hands in the puddle, then reached to cup some water from the drip.

'Wait!' said Beth. 'I heard water not out of a tap carries diseases.'

'And I *know* if someone doesn't drink something, they're dead in three days. Dad's taken me hiking in worse places than this.' He cupped his hands again and tried to fill them with the trickle. More dripped between his fingers than stayed in his web-coated palms—the webbing's uneven surface causing the leaks—but he had enough to drink.

Beth wondered how thirsty she was and looked down at her own hands. The sheer web-gloves covering them now showed patterns as well as lines connecting to the white band at her wrists, where a segmented circle continued to glow ominously. What did it mean?

Zane leant back and smacked his lips. 'I needed that. Can't be half dead from thirst if I'm to fight.'

'Fight? You mean another tree octopus-thing or those tribesmen?'

Zane shrugged. 'Both.'

'But the tribesmen didn't even attack us! We're the ones who ran into their camp and killed their mutt. What am I saying? *You* killed their mutt.'

'They attacked us. It wasn't my fault.'

'This is *all* your fault.' Tears stung Beth's eyes again. 'Who knows where we are, or how far from home, we've no way of getting back, and we're surrounded by who knows what!'

'Well, we do know what—they're the beastmen of Tordon and this is Tordon.' He gestured around them.

'No, Zane. This is nothing like Tordon. You can't *die* in Tordon. You can't get *these* in Tordon.' She jabbed at some deep scratches on her arm covered in dry blood. 'And now we're on the run from an entire tribe of, of people, for attacking them and killing their pet!'

'But remember that engraving on the tree? *Once a killing, twice the killing?*' Zane's eyes pleaded with her. 'I thought it meant to kill. It's so *much* like Tordon here, you've got to admit it. Look at the trees. And those beastmen wear the same stuff, and the mutts.'

'And the blood?'

He glanced at his own scratches. 'Well, no, not the blood.' He took a deep breath. 'I guess I got it wrong.' He looked up at the surrounding forest. 'This has to be one of the places that inspired Kaleski to create Tordon though.'

'Do you think?' Beth muttered sarcastically.

'So those rumours about him finding a dimensional gateway were true?' He paused. 'Which means there has to be a way back.'

Beth nodded. If Kaleski came here *and* got back home, it must be possible for them too. 'If we survive long enough,' she said miserably, scanning the bark of the trees as if one of them might contain a shiny black door. 'There has to be a way back, somewhere.'

A green lizard climbed onto a nearby branch, curling its tail so as to hug the branch, and cocked its head. She'd never seen a lizard like it before, so green and yet so— orange? It was changing colour like a chameleon. White stripes formed along its orange sides until they looked like lines ending in arrowheads. The lizard's big green eyes swirled and looked forward, following the direction of its streaks. Its tongue flicked that way too. Then its eyes swivelled back to stare directly at Beth before looking again in the direction of its arrows—towards the vertical rockface beyond the boulders. There was a flat ledge in the rockface, just above head height. Was the lizard trying to tell her something?

Slowly it changed colour again, until its body matched its surroundings, blending so completely it became invisible from tail to nose. Only its green eyes remained, as if floating in space. They looked at her briefly and winked, then disappeared too.

'Did you see that?' Beth whispered.

'What?' said Zane, washing the sweat from his hair.

As he pushed it back into its usual style, a terrible yet distant shriek pierced the air.

'Did you *hear* that? We should find somewhere safer,' Beth said, standing. 'How about up there?' She pointed to the flat ledge, pointed out by the lizard.

'And how are we supposed to get up there?'

'It's not that high.'

Zane rubbed his chin. 'Maybe. Might be difficult though. Could you pull yourself up there?'

'Could you?'

'What's that supposed to mean?' he snapped, sucking in his stomach. 'I'd probably beat you to the top! What do you think I am, a lazybones?'

Beth raised her eyebrows. 'We'll see.'

'We sure will.'

'Great, let's go.'

He didn't answer, just stood still eyeing the ledge.

'Something wrong?'

'Not keen on heights, that's all.'

Beth rolled her eyes, tucked her sword through her belt, moved around the boulders and found a sturdy bulge in the rockface. Another shriek sounded in the distance. She glanced back at Zane. 'Now's the time to get over it. What do you fear more—heights, vine-swinging monsters or angry beastmen?'

Zane searched the trees behind him, jittery, then eyed the ledge. 'I'll watch where you go first.'

'Fine.' She shook her head and heaved herself up to her first foothold. It was harder than she'd expected, especially with muddy shoes making the rock slippery. She was soon out of breath and struggling.

'A little to your right,' Zane said under his breath.

Beth saw the handhold he meant and pulled herself up, swinging a knee onto the ledge's flat top, then rolling herself up and on. 'Your turn,' she called down.

He took a deep breath, secured his sword and reached for the rockface. With one foot on the first bulge, he climbed well enough until he was halfway up. There, balancing on a particularly large bulge, he bounced as if about to launch himself upward, yet both feet remained firmly on the bulge.

'Here,' Beth said, securing herself and lowering her hand to help.

He ignored it and began climbing again, though his arms shook and he kept looking down.

'What's your dad do anyway?' Beth asked, thinking he needed a distraction.

'Navy marine,' he grunted, bitterness in his voice. 'Does stuff like this for fun.' His muddy feet slipped on a foothold.

She grabbed his shirt to help keep him steady. 'Stuff like what?'

'Obstacle courses. Survival camps. Rock climbing, like this! They all suck.'

'He takes you with him?'

'Unfortunately.' There, his feet caught the bulge.

Beth shuffled back. 'Sounds good to me—my dad prefers watching TV in the lounge room.'

Zane was almost at the top. 'So do I,' he huffed. 'It's where our computer lives. That's the problem.'

Zane's stats flashed in her mind. He played Tordon more than she did. If his dad really was a marine, he probably hated his son lazing at a computer all day.

Snap!

A twig broke nearby. Zane froze in fear and stared up

at Beth, his eyes huge. She reached down and grasped the back of his shirt again. Then another twig snapped, nearer this time. Beth stiffened and she could see Zane grit his teeth. He was concealed by long shadows cast by the surrounding trees—as long as he kept completely still.

How long could he stick there, though, without moving?

She closed her eyes tight and her fingers tighter as something moved closer.

Chapter 5

———

Footsteps shuffled, paused, then moved on. Lots of footsteps. Beth counted but lost track of her tally. The whole tribe seemed to be searching the forest together.

She waited until the last set of footsteps shuffled into the distance, then opened her eyes again. Pain lanced through her stiff fingers. Sweat poured down Zane's back and he was shaking uncontrollably. Then suddenly with a groan, he slid to the ground, down the rockface to land between the boulders, at the same time as the sound of sobbing rose from a nearby bush.

He immediately froze again with his back to the rockface.

The bush shook, then a tribesman stumbled out, crying. This close, his features looked almost human. In fact, when he removed his horned headdress to wipe his face and remove his fake tail so he could slump to the ground, he *was* human—as pale, and as much a kid as herself.

She narrowed her eyes. He also looked familiar. His red hair and blue eyes reminded her of someone from

Tordon, whose avatar always wore a leather necklace with a four-rods Rune of Death pendant. What was his name? Ah yes, DaveT. He had boasted to the chatroom that he'd made the necklace himself. This tribesman had the exact same necklace, and looked exactly like DaveT.

'DaveT?' Beth called, scrambling down the rockface to join Zane.

Zane scowled and elbowed her, but it was too late. The tribesman had seen them.

DaveT stepped closer and dragged his arm across his face. 'Who are you?'

'I'm BGwarrior—Beth. This is Zane007. I was at the bottom of The Chameleon Chart's top ten when you won last month.'

DaveT shook his head and sniffed. 'Last month? I won a few days ago.'

'Dude, you're confused,' said Zane.

Beth looked at Zane, willing him to be quiet. 'It doesn't matter. It only matters how we get home.'

'Home?' said DaveT. 'Do you know the way back? There was this flash of lightning or something, then I was here. The Witheng have been great and all, but...'

'The what?' snapped Zane.

'The Witheng tribesmen. But they don't know the way back home.'

'We're trying to find a way back ourselves,' said Beth. 'There's got to be a way, if this is where Kaleski got his inspiration for Tordon.'

'It is!' DaveT said, excited. 'I've seen him once, I think, looking for ideas.'

Beth nodded. 'Each new upgrade seems to have different stuff.'

'Moving between worlds for inspiration,' Zane gazed around him, 'what a way to live.'

'This,' Beth laughed, waving at her scratched and bloody arms, 'is no way to live!'

'It could be,' Zane screwed up his face. 'Better than being forced to march all day. What are you rushing home for anyway? To hang out with your loser dad?'

'He's not a loser.' Beth glared at him.

'It's not so bad here,' DaveT said, looking around. 'Look at these trees!'

'But you just said you want to go home.'

'I do now, because I lost Athul. The Witheng gave him to me after I learnt their ways.'

Beth stared in disbelief. 'But how could you have learnt their ways if you just got here?'

DaveT blinked. 'I never thought of that.' He blinked again. 'Still, I loved my mutt. He was my best friend, before he was killed.' He wiped his eyes. 'Murdered!'

'Best friend?' Beth repeated, a sinking feeling growing in her stomach. *Once a killing, twice a killing.* When a friend dies, it hurts those who loved them too.

'Yeah,' murmured DaveT, 'the mutts here are practically human. They have a unique language, simple to understand if you listen. Funny how they look exactly like those in Tordon. Much friendlier of course!' He sighed. 'The Witheng are taking Athul's body for burial while I hunt the killers.' He picked up his spear and shook it. 'It's my responsibility to find them, and kill them!' DaveT shook his spear again. 'Will you help me? If I don't find them, they'll attack our families in their sleep.' He looked worried.

Beth took a deep breath.

'Don't!' hissed Zane.

'DaveT,' she began, reaching to pat his hairy arm then thinking better of it, 'there aren't any killers.' She waited until he looked into her eyes. 'Zane…accidentally killed your mutt. And we're both very sorry. But the good news is: you don't have to keep hunting anyone.'

Zane groaned. 'Now you've done it.'

Beth ignored him. 'Go find your tribe and tell him they can sleep safe tonight. We're no danger to anyone.'

DaveT glanced at Zane, then back at Beth, anger clouding his expression.

'We thought your mutt was attacking us,' explained Beth quickly. 'It ran at us!'

DaveT backed away like she was a monster. 'It ran at you because he's friendly!'

'Everyone just calm down,' Zane said. 'This is just one big misunderstanding. We didn't know your mutt was friendly.'

'You killed Athul!' DaveT shouted. 'And you attacked my tribe? You?' He shook his head. 'Over here!' he shouted over his shoulder. 'I found them!'

'No, wait!' Beth said. 'You don't understand—we were scared!'

'We thought he was going to kill us!' said Zane.

'Kill you?' DaveT's face screwed up in disgust. 'He would never do that.'

'It looked like it to me.' Zane folded his arms. 'It was self-defence!'

'We were very confused,' Beth added. 'Please try to understand. Weren't you afraid when you first came here?'

DaveT's face crumpled and he looked away down the hillside. 'It's going to be cold tonight without Athul.'

Beth felt sick with guilt. 'Why don't you come with us?' she suggested. 'We're searching for a way back home and need your help. Do you know what these are, for instance?' She held up her hands.

DaveT stared at the sheer webbing coating his own hands. 'Mine are like that too. I forget they're there now.'

Beth squinted at the faint glow on his wristbands. 'But your circles aren't the same as ours. There are segments missing. Look, Zane,' she said, comparing their hands, 'they're diff…'

Snap!

The bushes rustled and Zane immediately reached for his sword, but wasn't fast enough. A Witheng tribesman pounced out pointing a spear. He had a feline look about him, with short horns protruding from his forehead.

'Wait!' cried DaveT.

The tribesman glared at him, but didn't lower his weapon. DaveT gestured for calm and they spoke to one side in low mutters. Beth hoped DaveT was explaining things properly.

More Witheng appeared, encircling them with spears. Two carried a heavy weight wrapped in white sackcloth— it had to be poor Athul. DaveT spoke quietly to them also, but Beth could only make out the occasional repeated phrase: *once a killing, twice the killing.*

'You should've kept quiet,' Zane hissed at her.

'But don't you think it's odd how DaveT has no idea of time passing?'

DaveT turned then and shook his head gravely. 'I regret to tell you this, but because you entered our camp and killed Mutt Athul…'

'For which,' Beth interrupted, 'we are really, really sorry.'

'…you are deemed guilty.'

The tribesman cheered.

DaveT thumped his spear on the ground. 'The Witheng have passed judgement—*once a killing, twice the killing.* We will execute you both.'

Chapter 6

'*What?*' Beth shouted at the tribesmen surrounding them in the forest dell. She stepped around the boulders towards DaveT. 'They can't kill us *both*! I didn't do anything!'

'There is an alternative,' DaveT pointed at Zane. '*You*, Beth, can execute *him*. If you take his life, it would fit the law.'

Beth glared at Zane. 'Don't tempt me!'

'But it was self defence!' Zane said, glaring back at Beth, then DaveT. 'Just like your tribe killed that tree-octopus thing.'

'That is different,' said DaveT, shuddering. 'And we didn't kill it, we only stopped it for now. That creature is an evil curse on the forest. It steals our strength and feeds on our children. We wound it, kill it, burn it, yet it returns more powerful than its last shape. It will return again and be even more deadly. At first it could only climb up and down the trees. Now it can swing between them on vines, even jump short distances over the ground. One day it will probably be able to run!'

'Okay, so how about,' Zane wiped his palms down his top, 'how about we slay your monster for you, once and for all, instead of you killing us—deal?'

Beth stared at Zane, lost for words.

DaveT's eyes widened. 'You want to slay the Hupuleq for us? It's impossible!'

'At least it gives us a fighting chance! Better than a straight-out execution, right Beth?'

'Um,' Beth murmured, blinking. Executions? Slayings? What kind of place was this? Of course she couldn't kill Zane, but fighting an indestructible monster?

Taking her silence as agreement, DaveT turned to the Witheng, but apart from their shocked expressions, they seemed impressed with Zane's offer. The horned tribesman stepped forward.

'We agree. Your lives will be spared if you destroy the Hupuleq curse. This obeys our law. But there is one condition—he must witness the battle.' He pointed at DaveT.

'Agreed,' said Zane.

Beth's mouth gaped open as her thoughts tumbled around. She had to get away! Perhaps without all the Witheng watching, they could escape? DaveT wouldn't really make *her* fight a monster, would he? She took a steadying breath, repeating Kumdo's philosophy in her mind—*discipline, concentration, endurance*. She needed to keep a cool head.

Zane muttered something about needing weapons and Beth nodded. They'd need weapons so they could *pretend* they were going to kill this thing. DaveT took some of the Witheng's spears as Zane swung his sword around like he was warming up his muscles. Beth knew he was showing off, but it worked. The crowd was impressed.

DaveT blinked then, his expression changing, lifting as if seeing them for the first time. 'Do I know you?'

Beth smiled. 'Yes, it's Beth and Zane.'

DaveT frowned until the feline tribesman stamped his spear on the ground. 'We must hurry. Lately, each of the Hupuleq's new shapes have been more horrible, vicious and deadly than the one before. It's attracted by blood, so we must first bury our dead.'

Beth glanced at the wrap covering Athul's body and the red, wet stain seeping over it.

'This way.' DaveT gestured down the slope and they moved off.

The tree canopy above them was green and lush, yet it hid so many deadly secrets. Had forests always been this way? Is that why they were farmed back home?

At the bottom of the slope, DaveT veered left. 'Our burial place is just along the stream.'

The sound of rushing water was close. They rounded a mossy bend to see a magnificent waterfall gush from the hillside just in front of them, crashing with thunder onto rocks below. A rippling stream flowed out and sparkled in the late afternoon sun. Further along, another water source rushed from between the trees to join the stream, and where the two streams joined was an enormous roiling pool, its dark water laced with foam.

'This is our burial place,' DaveT told them. 'The Gateway. The Witheng believe it leads to the next life. Don't slip though. If you fall, the Gateway quickens so we can't rescue you.'

Gateway? Beth wondered, then sniffed. There was an odd odour—fresh, but at the same time metallic, like overheated wires? She sniffed again. When her dad had worked for the tree farm years ago, he'd brought home some work equipment to weld in the shed. She remembered sparks flying as he melted metal together, and this same sort of smell.

Four tribesmen, DaveT among them, shifted along the mossy banks of the pool, holding Athul's sackcloth-wrapped body. Once they'd reached a rocky ledge sticking out over the water, the bearers lifted the body high and the Witheng sang a short guttural tune before dropping their burden into the whirling currents. As soon as it hit, the pool swirled faster and faster, then flashed white, nearly blinding them.

Beth blinked.

DaveT walked back to Beth and Zane as they stood rubbing their eyes. 'Athul will be released from his body now to live again.'

'Did you see that flash?' Beth whispered to Zane. 'What if this isn't a gateway to an afterlife, but to another world—our world? Remember earlier, when DaveT said he'd seen a flash when he arrived here? I swear I saw a flash too, when we fell through Kaleski's front door. This could be our way back home!'

Zane stared downward. 'Looks like a whirlpool to me.'

'Dave,' said Beth, 'tell us more about this place?'

'The water has healing powers, that's all I know. The Gateway leads to the next life where the souls of the dead are healed.'

'Don't you think it's strange the Witheng use the word "gateway"?' She looked around the forest. 'Couldn't it be a —'

Before she could finish her sentence, the Witheng started pointing and shouting at the treetops. With a shriek, a huge tentacled monstrosity dropped among them, landing on the tribesmen who'd carried Athul into the water. Its scaly-plated new body crushed them instantly. Even though it was bigger than before, with more tentacles, Beth could tell this was the same creature. It gave her the same sick feeling in her stomach.

The Witheng threw their spears, but their weapons bounced off its impenetrable scales. It humped across to a hanging vine, gripped it and hauled itself up, for a moment revealing a soft underbelly. Once suspended, however, it moved quickly again, slashing tentacles lined with claws at one tribesman and then another. They screamed and the rest of the tribe scattered into the trees, crying out in panic. Only DaveT, Beth and Zane were left behind, standing away from the trees near the water.

For a moment the monster clung in the trees, watching them with its multiple eyes.

'It can't move fast without vines,' whispered Beth. She wondered how far it could jump. 'Hey!' she screamed.

'Over here!'

'What are you doing?' hissed Zane.

'We need to get it off the vines. I saw its belly before—it's soft!'

He shook his head. 'It's all too much. *Too* much!'

Beth gripped her sword. This was no time to fall apart. 'When it jumps down to attack us, hit it from underneath.'

Zane puffed his cheeks and crept forward, holding out a shaking spear.

'Ready, DaveT?' Beth said, before taking a deep breath and screaming as loud as she could.

The Hupuleq's eyes rolled wildly. It lengthened its tentacles, producing sharp talons at their ends.

She yelled again and it leapt towards them like a toad, landing nearby but not close enough to attack. Beth spied the same soft patch of underbelly before it prepared to pounce again.

'Ready?' she yelled, re-gripping her sword.

It sprang, forcing them to crouch under its swiping limbs. Beth aimed a jab at its underside as a spear thrust past her, striking the same place. DaveT gave a triumphant war cry as the creature slumped sideways, bleeding.

'We did it!' yelled Zane.

Beth grinned, until the blood oozing from the creature's side solidified and grew into a scaly new tentacle. Its body spasmed as it pulled itself upright.

'Now!' yelled DaveT. 'While it's still weak!'

Beth ran forward, jabbing the Hupuleq as Zane swung his sword to slice the new tentacle in half, then whatever else he could reach. Soon they were sweating and huffing among a mess of hairy tentacles, scales and blood. It looked like they'd diced the creature enough to fill some giant's chunky steak pie.

'Awesome!' Zane panted, surveying his handiwork. 'Who's lazy now, eh Dad?'

Beth shook her head. Whatever fantasy Zane was living right now, dicing monsters was not her idea of exercise. Nor had it worked. 'Watch out!' she screamed as the monster regrew new tentacles, as well as a second mouth of piercing fangs.

'Let it come!' Zane bellowed, hacking at another limb. 'No wonder Kaleski got his inspiration from here! This is epic.'

'But look what you're doing!' Beth shouted. Four tentacles were already eight, rapidly changing into sixteen. If Zane kept going, soon there'd be over fifty. 'You're making it worse!' Wait, maybe that's what the engraving meant? Kill something once here, and you only have to kill it again, twice as much and twice as hard. 'Zane, you've got to stop!'

'But I can chop them all!'

'Look!' she screamed, pointing as the monster grew larger, its arms forming quicker and longer.

Zane's expression shifted. 'How…?'

'That's what I've been trying to tell you!'

He leapt back as the monster became a mass of whirling tentacles, slowly cutting off any escape. They backed toward the whirlpool.

'Go for the eyes!' DaveT shouted. 'At least if it's blinded, we can retreat!'

Retreat sounded good. Though as DaveT rushed forward, the huge creature dodged and one of its tentacles slipped into the pool. The tentacle melted where it touched the water, releasing a strong stench of burning electricity. Both the creature's mouths widened in an ear-wrenching shriek.

'Look!' Zane pointed with his sword. 'The water hurts it!'

It pulled its shrivelled tentacle out of the pool, and backed away from the waterhole. Nothing grew back in the tentacle's place.

'Herd it into the water!' Beth yelled, splashing water at the creature until it let them past.

Zane charged at it, trying to drive it towards the whirlpool, but its sharp sickle-fingers came in fast and slashed across his chest.

'Argh!' he cried, dropping to his knees and clutching the deep wound. Blood ran through his fingers.

'No!' screamed Beth, driving her sword deep into its side, though from the wound emerged sharp horns. This was impossible!

It shifted around to face her, its talons catching on DaveT, giving him a horrible gash across his back. He lurched to one side, then tumbled straight into the whirlpool. It flashed white and he was gone.

'DaveT!' Beth yelled, gripping her sword harder. Zane was still lying on the ground. It was down to her. She had to get it into the water—but how? Blood attracts it, she remembered. 'Zane!' she yelled, 'get in the water!'

'It's a whirlpool, Beth!'

'I know!' She crept back towards Zane, eyeing the creature as it followed. 'But DaveT said the water has healing powers and he called the Hupuleq a curse—curses can't be killed, but they can be healed! That's the only way to get rid of it!' She helped Zane to his feet, then edged back towards the rocky ledge where the tribesmen had taken Athul. 'You can swim can't you? When I say go, jump.'

'What, and *hope* it'll follow us in? Whoa,' Zane cried, slipping on the mossy surface of the ledge and dropping his sword. As it fell into the water, the pool's sides smoothed and glowed as its churning waters sparkled gold.

'Did you see that? Quick, drop your spear in too!' she told Zane.

'Are you mad?'

'Just do it!' She held her own sword out over the golden-glowing water and with a deep breath, tossed it into the centre. The pool's radiance brightened and a static charge surged in the air. 'This is it. Ready?'

Zane shook his head, clutching at his bloodstained top. He'd scrunched it up over his gash as a kind of compress.

'Blood attracts it,' she gestured at his top. 'We only need to wait.' She positioned herself and Zane closer to the water's edge before turning to face the monster. It had crouched low and bared all its fangs. 'Let go of your top, Zane.'

Zane whimpered, then let go of his top so his wound bled freely.

The monster's eyes glowed green, then it sprang, aiming for the wound.

'Now!' Beth cried and pulled Zane back with all her strength.

They hit the water, which brightened yet again, and the Hupuleq sailed over them, its front tentacles splayed outward, searching, while its back tentacles scrabbled for the ledge's sides. But with the sides of the pool smoothed and mossy, the creature couldn't find any grip and it slipped, plunging into the water along with them.

They hit the churning wet and began spinning, the creature shrieking in agony as its body shrivelled and disintegrated. The whirlpool rushed around them and Beth had to fight not to drown in its roiling currents. The pool's centre was black and deep. What had she been thinking? She went to take a breath and got a mouthful of water. Ahead of her, Zane's head bobbed as the current dragged them apart. His head kept sinking and resurfacing like he was trying to swim but didn't have the strength.

Then he went totally under.

Was it the Hupuleq? She looked around. Behind her floated a vanishing mess of scales, fur and tentacles, slowly sinking under golden waters. The only sound now was the roaring of the whirlpool, which twisted her faster and faster, despite her kicking away. She was so tired already—she couldn't fight it anymore, and as liquid covered her nose, she held her breath and sank.

Why had she done this? Why had she met a bunch of strangers outside a derelict house, entered another world, fought the worst monster imaginable, and now jumped into a whirlpool? Her father would never know what had happened to her, her body lost to the deep golden-flecked water.

A bright light flashed, blinding her, and she blinked.

Everything was dazzling and bright, but not wet anymore. Then, with a jarring thump, she landed on solid ground. She gasped air, and lots of dust, enough to make her cough. But there was no more water. She wasn't drowning, instead sitting and breathing. She looked around. Golden flecks still swirled everywhere but, instead of water, she was surrounded by spinning sand.

Chapter 7

—

Dry, hard, biting sand flew all around and stung Beth's eyes, roaring like a tribe. She put up her hands to shield her face but she was surrounded by it, covered in it—it was in her hair, nose and ears. She couldn't be home. At home, now trees were largely contained on farms, open patches of loose top soil often blew into raging dust storms. But they never had *sand* storms. They were somewhere new. *They?* Zane was nowhere in sight.

'Zane!' she coughed as grains of sand scratched the inside of her throat. She peered between her fingers, trying to see. 'Zane!' Some way off was a dark blurred patch. Was it him? She shuffled over. 'Zane!' The sand spun around her in spirals and circles like a mini hurricane but, yes, it was him.

'I can't see!' Zane shouted and coughed.

'Get down!' Beth crouched to escape the harsh grit pounding her face.

Zane staggered up instead, his hands outstretched as if searching for something. He stepped forward though the wind blasted him backwards.

'Where are you going?' Beth shouted. 'If we stick together we might get home!' She heard nothing except winds whistling and grains of sand thrashing each other. She crawled forward, partly covering her eyes with a hand. Her face and body stung. 'Zane!'

He was standing, hugging himself and leaning into the wind.

Still on her hands and knees, she tugged at his ankles until he fell onto his knees.

'Ouch, Beth!' he shouted, clutching them. 'I saw rocks over there!'

She looked to where he was pointing. 'Okay! But you can see more clearly down here! Let's go!'

They crawled forward together from rock to rock, getting some protection from the harsh wind.

'Sorry about your knees,' Beth said, once they'd settled between the biggest rocks. 'I was trying to get you out of the wind.'

'They're fine,' Zane said, clasping his chest instead where the monster had wounded him.

'Is it serious?'

'How would I know?' Zane snapped, moving his hand so she could look. His top was torn and blood had seeped into the fabric, but the wound itself was no longer bleeding.

'That Hupuleq gave you quite a slashing,' Beth peered closer, 'but it's formed a scab already, somehow. Must have been that water's healing powers. That's good.'

'Good?' Zane spat in the sand beside him. 'I almost

died! Now we're who-knows-where, in the middle of who-knows-what!'

'Don't you think I know that!' Beth yelled, staring out into the storm. The whirlpool had been a gateway, but it hadn't taken them home. 'Can you see DaveT?'

'No. I haven't seen anyone other than you.' He spat more sand out of his mouth.

Beth screwed up her face. 'Keep your bodily fluids to yourself.'

'Only if you wipe your nose.'

'What? Oh.' She hadn't realised her eyes and nose were streaming from all the sand.

Zane gave her a look and turned his back.

Fine. There was nothing to say or do anyway until the wind died down. It took a while, but slowly the sandstorm faded. Hawks shrieked in the distance, then the sky cleared. Finally Beth could see further than a few metres—ten metres, then fifty, then a hundred—until she could see nothing but sandy desert, rolling dunes, and a sky so blue and clear. Not a speck of haze, pollution or dust—a foreign sky. With a hot, hot sun.

Beth tugged at her short sleeves.

'So thirsty!' moaned Zane, standing to look around.

'Would you rather be drowning in a whirlpool?'

Ignoring her, he squinted into the harsh light. 'Great, nothing for miles.'

She stood to look. 'Could be something over that dune there. Should we go see?'

'*You* can.'

Beth was about to tell him what he could go and do, when the sound of thudding hooves pounded towards them, followed by voices shouting. Five mounted desert warriors were surrounding the outcrop. Curved daggers, heavily jewelled, hung from belts around their waists. They wore long white robes and their eyes were only just visible through the red-chequered wrap covering their heads.

One of them jumped from his horse and unwound his face scarf to reveal a jagged scar across his cheek. 'Strangers!' he called, striding toward them.

The other warriors leapt off their horses in unison and marched closer.

'Who are you?' the scarred warrior yelled. 'This land belongs to Sheikh Zidan! You are not permitted here.'

'We,' Beth stammered as the leader neared, 'we didn't know.'

The scar on his face twitched. 'Then you must come to the sheikh's palace.'

'That scar,' Zane said, pointing, 'I recognise it from somewhere. Don't I know you?'

The leader's eyes narrowed, then he signalled to his men. 'Fetch them.'

The warriors dashed as one to the outcrop.

'Get off!' Zane shouted, kicking sand as they grabbed him.

'Don't touch me!' Beth screamed. But the warriors were stronger and threw them over their shoulders before lugging them back to the horses.

'It is the wish of Sheikh Zidan,' said the leader as Beth

was slung into his saddle. He leapt up behind her, took up the reins and turned his mount around.

Hot horse and leather blasted Beth's nose as she tried wriggling free. From the corner of her eye, she saw Zane squirming in another saddle. 'Let me go!'

The leader just heeled his horse into a gallop. 'Ai ai ai!'

The warriors took off across the desert at a cracking pace. Beth gripped the saddle, breathless.

They rode across the dunes and paused at the highest. A desert city appeared below them, with five towers of a palace jutting high within its walls. Water glittered beyond and, as they zigzagged down the dune, Beth saw a rocky coastline framing a small port. Five large boats bobbed on the water, pale against the blue.

Once on flat ground again, the horses sped up, riding side by side. Beth glanced at the horse beside her. Its mane had five coloured ribbons braided through it and on the hilt of the warrior's sword, a large five-sided emerald glinted in the sun. Five men, five towers, five boats and five ribbons. Beth narrowed her eyes. Now a five-sided emerald. It couldn't be coincidence. Something was written on each sword's scabbard too. She strained to make out the engraving as the horse galloped at a steady pace.

A gem without gratitude is grievous.

Beth committed the phrase to memory, repeating it in her mind. The last inscription they'd seen, on that forest tree, had had a direct effect on their safety.

The desert city's gates loomed ahead, vast and wooden as five sentries ushered the warriors through.

Beth glimpsed the colourful hubbub of a crowded marketplace—the delicious scent of fried food and spices wafting across as they entered a large courtyard bordering some military barracks. The warriors dismounted, and Zane and Beth slid off the horses, Zane clutching his chest.

'Water?' the scar-faced leader asked them, holding up a clay jug.

Beth nodded her thanks and sipped it gratefully. While she drank, he shouted instructions to his men who led the horses into some stables. At his waist, his dagger's magnificent emerald glinted in the sunlight. Without thinking, she reached to touch it. A tingling raced through her fingers ending in her thumb, which turned bright green.

'What on earth?' she murmured. She turned her hand over and back. Was it the webbing that turned green, or her skin underneath? She wriggled her fingers. It felt okay. In fact, it felt kind of nice.

She handed the jug back to the warrior and he smiled fleetingly.

'You,' he said to Zane. 'Water?'

Zane peered at him. 'You look really familiar. Aren't you that gamer, Jumbie? You got that scar when your brother hit you with a toy train. You said so in the chatroom.'

The warrior shook his head. 'I am of the tribe of Sheikh Zidan. I won this scar in battle.'

Zane huffed, snatched the jug, then splashed its contents all over his face, shaking the water from his hair. He eyed the emerald, then reached out to touch it too.

'No!' The warrior swiped his hand away. 'Do not touch the emerald of Zidan!' He glared at Zane and his scar twitched until one of his riders appeared holding some white robes. 'Put these on while I inform the sheikh you have entered our land.' He eyed them both. 'He decides whether strangers rescued from sandstorms are welcome, or not.' And with that he strode away with his men, gesturing for the city gates to be locked.

'I wonder what they do with strangers who *aren't* welcome,' said Beth, climbing into her robe.

'Eat them,' Zane snapped.

Beth gnashed her teeth. 'I don't think they like you much either. Did you read the engravings on their scabbards? I think emeralds might be important here, and the number five.'

'Or equally unimportant,' Zane growled, shoving on his robe.

'Emeralds *are* important, Zane. Look!' She showed him her thumb. It was still green.

'Ergh, is that infected?'

'No, it's from touching the emerald. I had to touch it,' she said, shrugging before wandering toward a low wall.

'You're crazy—just like DaveT and Jumbie—another Tordon gamer gone nuts.' Zane looked over the wall into the marketplace. 'Stay here if you want but I'm escaping. Check it out!'

Beneath them spread the markets. Five hawks were leashed to a mud-washed wall, beyond which merchants haggled from stalls, shouting their trade. Camels spat as they were inspected and prodded. Goats and sheep bleated for attention and proud stallions whinnied while being fitted with beaded bridles. Beyond the animals hundreds of people milled about, wearing the same white robes as Beth and Zane now wore. They could easily disappear among the crowds and continue their search for home. If they stayed, who knew what Sheikh Zidan would decide?

'Okay,' Beth agreed. 'We can merge with the crowd through there, see?' She pointed to an archway through which a constant stream of people moved. 'But no running—with these robes on we'll look like everyone else.'

Zane pulled himself up onto the wall, holding his chest. 'Okay, but follow me. Do exactly as I say.'

She huffed, pointing to his chest. Blood had seeped onto his robe again. 'What about that?'

Zane glanced down and paled. 'It was the horse ride.'

'You need a bandage.'

'Well, there are none here.' And he slid off the wall onto the other side.

Beth hauled herself up and over, then followed him down a few steps into a dim passageway that merged with another tunnel. Soon they were stepping into sunlight under the archway and among a steady flow of people.

'Help us! Help us!' came a cry.

Sitting against a wall, several men in rags held their hands out for money.

'Zane, look at their wrists!' Around each of the beggar's wrists was a white band, just like the bands that had appeared on her and Zane's wrists when they fell through Kaleski's door, although the webbing on their hands wasn't so obvious now. She held out one of her wrists and pointed at a band.

Zane peered at the beggars' wrists and stepped towards them. 'Can you help us? Are you trying to get home as well?'

The beggars smiled toothlessly.

'Home?' said one. 'The dirt I sit on is my home. How about some coins?'

'But you have the same wristbands as us.' Zane held out his hand.

'All I see is skin. Now, give us money!'

Beth stepped forward. 'But you must have come from somewhere, like us!'

'The dirt is my home—always has been, always will be.'

'Yes,' said another beggar, his voice cracking, 'we want nothing more than the dirt. The dirt is our friend.'

'Or will be,' cackled another, 'once you give us coins.' He lurched to grab Zane's wrist.

'You're demented,' Zane said, backing away.

'Come back!'

'Give us coins!'

Beth hurried into the crowd with Zane at her heels. 'Our bands were invisible to them!'

'I know. Creepy. Quick, this way,' he pointed between some stalls.

The markets were like a maze, with people constantly stopping to view the stallholders' wares—tasselled camel saddles, palm leaf rope, woven curtains and horns.

Zane took a side turn down an alley where there were even more people and stalls.

'Where are you going?' Beth demanded. 'We won't get far down there.'

'I'm looking for a way out.'

'More like deeper in. We should go that way.'

'No, every time I listen to you...' Zane paused as his eyes lit up. 'Whoa, look at this!' He stepped towards a huge collection of rifles, ammunition and knives. 'Fine looking weapons. My father would like these.' He picked one up.

Beth rolled her eyes until she spied the next stall. 'Look at all this jewellery for sale!'

'There's lots of everything for sale.'

'Yeah, but these are amazing!' Beads and chains knotted with cloves, bells, turquoise, coins and cucumber-shaped amulets that rattled with tiny seeds. Beside them sat a tray full of gems—pentagons in every colour. Beth stood mesmerised, thinking of the warrior's emeralds. As she did, she reached for a ring set with five green stars.

A gem without gratitude is grievous.

'We're not here for the shopping,' Zane hissed before she could touch any. 'I'm going this way. Bye.'

'Wait!' she said, annoyed. 'Remember my thumb? Remember the engraving? *A gem without gratitude is grievous?*'

'What are you talking about? Not emeralds again!'

'Yes, no... Wait, what's that smell?'

Smoky-sweet incense burnt the air. Beside the gem stall was a tent, in front of which sat an old woman fanning a tiny flame with a small piece of leather. Rings decorated every finger and heavy silver jewellery hung from her neck. She looked like a fortune-teller. Her black headdress was decorated with silver beads and her piercing green eyes peered through slits in the material.

Zane stared too and the woman gazed back, noticing his blood-spotted robe. Then her gaze shifted behind them to some commotion.

Beth turned. Warriors were moving fast through the crowd, shouting and spinning market-sellers around to see their faces.

Their absence had finally been noticed.

Z.F. Kingbolt

Chapter 8

Beth scanned the desert market stalls for a place to hide. Sheikh Zidan's men would spot them any moment. The woman in the black headdress watched them, then leant back and raised the flap of her tent. With a wink, she gestured them inside.

Beth hesitated. Dried blood was smeared down the fabric of the tent. She wrinkled her nose and Zane shook his head.

The woman's eyes danced with laughter. 'Do not worry, no one has been harmed here. This,' she gestured at the blood, 'is the mark of a good host. If a guest is grateful for shelter and food, they wipe their hands from the lamb stew here.' She stood and waved them inside, pointing to five fat cushions strewn on a colourful carpet. 'Sit and rest. They will not find you here.'

Even with louder shouting behind them, Zane hesitated.

'Zane, it's a place to hide!' Beth took a deep breath, then stepped inside the tent. 'Thank you,' she whispered to the woman.

With a huff, Zane ducked after her and the woman followed, pulling the tent flaps shut behind them.

'Thank you,' Beth said again to the woman, then sat on a cushion and stared at Zane sitting and grumbling to himself as he plucked at his robe.

'Zane,' Beth hissed while the woman clattered among her pots, tutting every time she glanced at Zane. 'Say thank you.'

'But I don't want to be in here,' he said. 'It stinks.'

'Why are you so ungrateful?' Then her face lit up. 'Un*grateful*. It's a warning!'

'What?'

'The engraving: A gem *without* gratitude is grievous. Being hidden in here is a gift for us—precious as any gem—and this nice woman is putting herself in danger by helping us. Not being grateful probably causes her grief.'

'So?'

'So the last time you didn't pay attention to an engraving, you almost got us killed.'

The woman turned. 'It is wise to heed all warnings given us in life. Warnings come from others who have tried and failed.' She smiled humbly. 'I need more herbs for your wound.' She left the tent with a washing pot.

Zane crossed his legs, looking embarrassed. He glanced at Beth, then snorted. 'My whole life is a warning to others.'

'Why?'

'You know,' he shrugged, picking at his cushion. 'I love gaming—it's my life, but Dad thinks it's a waste of time.

He wants me to be more like him, some big hero.' He shrugged again. 'Every weekend we have to do survival stuff—as if I'm ever going to need it! I'll never be like him.'

Beth pressed her lips together. They could have used some survival stuff lately.

'But I'll show him I don't need it,' Zane said. 'One day I'll work for Ripple, develop my own games.'

Beth shrugged. 'Not everyone's cut out for the military.'

He glanced at her. 'I could have shown him if I'd won The Chameleon Chart, which is exactly what I was going to do before you went and wrecked it all.'

Beth stuck out her chin.

'Anyway,' Zane sighed, 'we should probably get going. Those warriors are bound to have passed by now.'

'But your wound!'

'I need to get out of here.' He reached for the tent flap.

Beth scrambled after him. One thing was certain—there was no gateway in this tent, no whirlpool or black door.

But before they could step outside, the woman in the headdress entered, her hands full of herbs. 'You are not staying?'

'I have to go,' said Zane, blinking in the dazzling sunlight beyond her.

'But we are very grateful for your help,' said Beth, nodding politely, 'and your words of wisdom.'

The woman nodded in return, then held out a clenched fist, turned it over and opened her hand. On her outstretched palm was a small pentagonal emerald.

Instinctively Beth reached to touch it. As her flesh connected with the surface of the gem, it tingled and the same flash of energy passed through her. When she looked down at her hand, the first finger glowed green next to her thumb. She gasped. 'Emeralds *are* important here!'

'An emerald hand begets freedom,' said the woman. 'Remember my words.'

Zane scowled at the woman, swiped at the tent curtain and stomped outside.

Beth wanted to apologise for his behaviour but he was fast disappearing into the crowd. And then she thought, *so*? He hadn't even looked back. Let him figure stuff out alone and see how far he'd get. She'd find home much easier on her own anyway.

She nodded goodbye to the woman and slipped into the busy market, wondering where she'd find more emeralds. She wasn't sure if they *would* get her home, but it was her only lead so far. She searched the stalls heading in the opposite direction to Zane—until there was a sudden shout behind her.

She spun around to see him crashing through the crowd towards her. 'Run!' he shouted in her face.

Sheikh Zidan's warriors were chasing right behind. They'd been spotted!

Together again, they dodged around carts and animals, merchandise and people, racing away from the warriors until a bag of grain spilled across their path. Zane slipped and crashed sideways into a stall of copper pots and pans, cymbals and bells. He yelled and clutched at his chest.

'Come on!' said Beth, hauling him up.

Zane shook her off and skidded on the grains again. The clang of falling metal echoed across the square as he knocked the stall into complete disarray. He stumbled and bumped into an old lady carrying a wicker basket. Both of them fell to the ground.

The old lady winced as she tried to get up.

Seeming to forget the warriors for a moment, Zane grabbed the old lady's basket and helped her up before gently steering her around a corner out the crowds' way. He even brushed off the basket as Beth quickly returned its contents.

'My grandma has one like it,' he mumbled.

The old lady bobbed her head, smiling with gratitude in her eyes. Then she took his hand and cupped both of hers over it, showing him her gleaming emerald ring.

Zane blinked and put his left hand over the ring. 'My thumb!' He smiled as it turned green.

'Feels good, I know,' said Beth.

Zane nodded as the old lady squeezed his hand, then released it and shuffled away.

'Strangers! Stop!' came a voice behind them.

Large hands gripped Beth's arms and yanked her backwards. She struggled, but it was useless—the warrior with the twitching scar had her firmly in his grasp.

Chapter 9

The market crowd parted in silence as the warriors marched Zane and Beth along the streets to Sheikh Zidan's palace. They passed through a wide square with five fountains and at the far end they faced heavy wooden doors, two metres tall and studded with brass and gems. The doors opened as they arrived, and they entered a smaller courtyard, its edges furnished with brightly coloured rugs. In the far corner, a fire crackled in a hearth and a round teapot steamed on a low table. A large man stepped from the shadows to greet them.

'The Sheikh Zidan!' announced the scar-faced warrior before bowing and moving back to stand by the wooden doors.

'Peace be with you,' said the sheikh, stretching out his arms. Like his warriors, he wore a white robe and a red-chequered headscarf tied by a black rope.

'What's peace to you?' muttered Zane. 'You're holding us against our will.'

Sheikh Zidan closed his bright green eyes, took a deep breath, then opened them again. 'Please, sit down,' he said calmly, gesturing to the cushions where he sat by the table. 'Let me serve you some tea.'

'So you can poison us? I don't think so,' Zane snarled, though he slumped down, gripping his chest.

Beth noticed the fresh blood there as she sat too.

'No, I must taste the tea before my guests. It is our tradition,' Sheikh Zidan said, pouring a thin liquid flecked with green bits into three thimble-sized cups.

Zane snorted. 'Guests.'

'Ah, but you *are* my guests, for I have used the greeting of travellers.' He sipped his own tea. 'When travellers pass on their desert journeys, a host may invite them in with a greeting of "peace be with you". If a traveller replies "with you be peace", they accept their host's hospitality and will do their family no harm. The two may even be enemies, but a guest today may be a host tomorrow.' He gestured at the tea. 'As strangers in these lands, I realise you must be on an important journey. So please, rest and refresh yourself.'

He waited for Zane pick up his tea.

'Baah!' Zane spat out the sip he'd taken.

The sheikh laughed a gentle, amused laugh. 'My sons, who are not yet ten years, act older than you! It is the way of the desert that children must behave as grown-ups, for if I were not here my young sons would be your host, offering you a meal and a place to sleep. Are you not yet grown, Zane?'

Zane glared at the sheikh. 'You sound like my father.'

The sheikh laughed and looked expectantly at Beth.

She sipped her tea and coughed at its strong mint taste,

yet still managed to swallow. It was so sweet though, she couldn't stomach anymore. 'Thank you, but could I have some water please?'

The sheikh smiled with approval. He picked up a brass tumbler and a water jug, poured some out and handed it to her.

'Thank you,' she said, and as she took the tumbler she saw its rim was decorated in tiny emerald shards. As soon as she touched it, she felt a tingle and a familiar energy course through her. Her right pinky finger turned green. Grinning, she wiggled her finger at Zane. The woman in the tent had said 'an emerald hand begets freedom'. With three of her fingers now green, perhaps freedom would soon be hers and she'd finally get home.

Zane raised his eyebrows, then cleared his throat. 'May I also have some water, please?'

With raised eyebrows, the sheikh passed him a fresh tumbler.

As Zane said the words 'thank you' and gulped down the water, the pinky finger on his left hand turned a glimmering green. Smiling, he wiped his mouth. 'I think I'm getting the hang of this.'

'And now,' the sheikh said, beckoning the scar-faced warrior forward. 'I see you have a wound that needs tending. I will see you both again at dinner.'

'Thank you,' Beth said, standing.

As they were escorted from the courtyard, Zane whispered. 'Perhaps manners are enough to confuse the old goat and get us out of here.'

'It's not just about manners,' Beth whispered back.

'Gratitude comes from the heart and I'll easily beat you there.'

'Who says?'

'I do.'

The scar-faced warrior showed them a washroom between two large airy rooms. In each room, a single bed was made up on a rug floor, and a fresh set of robes rested across the sheets. 'You will change and wash,' the warrior said to Beth. Then he pointed at Zane. 'But you will come with me.'

Zane's eyes widened, though he still followed the warrior out.

Beth took a set of robes into the washroom and splashed cold water on her face and arms, then changed into the new clothes. When she was ready, she waited by the window in her room feeling refreshed. The view was of a small treeless courtyard, which reminded her of home—except for the evening sky. Five enormous pink moons hung there, rather than the single one she was used to seeing. She sighed and turned away. Had Dad noticed she was missing yet? Who would get him his dinner? Who would make sure he had enough blankets when he fell asleep watching television? She began pacing the room. She had to find the way back home, and soon.

It was dark by the time Zane materialised in a fresh robe, his wound dressed and his hair wet.

'Did you get a make-over?' she asked, grumpily.

'Ha ha. No, I've been quizzing Jumbie.'

'The scar-faced warrior?'

'He's Jumbie, Beth—just like DaveT was DaveT. He's got bands on his wrists and everything, but when I asked him about it he refused to believe he might be from anywhere other than here. In fact, he said he'd cut me again if I mentioned it one more time.'

Beth chewed on a strand of her hair. 'Maybe he's been here so long he's forgotten, like DaveT? I hope the same doesn't happen to us.'

'It won't,' Zane said, though a worried frown crossed his face.

Beth looked away. She didn't want her memories to fade. She didn't want to forget how she got here, her Dad and home.

A young girl with dark hair came in and smiled shyly. 'I am Kira. You are to come and relax while we prepare dinner.'

She led them into a large courtyard lit with lamps. To one side was a bustling kitchen where several girls and boys were kneading dough. Kira pointed at some soft rugs nearby before trotting off to help. Lively tambourine and flute-like music penetrated the darkness, coming from the city outside.

Zane wandered over to a chess match where Jumbie was playing against a young boy. Zane whispered something to the boy who nodded before making his next move. A few moves later, he won the game. Onlookers laughed and slapped Zane's back as the boy leapt up to shake his hand. Another of Zane's fingers must have turned green because he held up his hand and waved it at Beth. She raised her eyebrows. Perhaps he was finally learning.

Watching the kitchen again, Beth was amazed at how expertly Kira worked her dough paper-thin. She then spread each one over a curved metal sheet balanced on the fire. So much dough and no microwave ovens. It was a world away from the delivery van arriving with dinner. She shuffled over to Kira.

'Can I help?'

Smiling, Kira passed her some dough, but it wasn't easy to mould into shape. It took her ages to get even one serving on the metal sheet. Kira giggled at her efforts and soon Beth was giggling too.

When the first batch of crisped flatbreads was ready, Beth helped hand them out. She snorted as Zane stuffed the warm bread in his mouth.

'I'm starving!' he mumbled as an explanation.

'Thirsty?' Kira asked Beth, offering her a bowl of something warm to drink.

Beth thanked her and the young girl smiled, making sure Beth's hand touched her emerald ring. Beth's middle finger tingled and turned green. Kira wiggled her own hand and Beth gasped—Kira's thumb turned green too!

She was about to ask why, when a deep voice interrupted behind her.

'I'm glad you are enjoying our hospitality,' Sheikh Zidan said. 'The stew is ready now. Let us eat together.' Kira shuffled away as he led them to a large open tent set up in a corner.

A group of cooks brought platters piled high with rice and chunks of meat covered in swirls of brown and white sauce. The warriors followed and sat at low tables on the carpets around them.

'Looks like puke,' Zane whispered to Beth, before thanking the sheikh. 'Smells good!'

'Enjoy. It is goat in spiced yoghurt sauce.'

'Goat? Like goats in the market?' Beth stammered. 'I thought yoghurt went with fruit.'

Sheikh Zidan shook his head. 'You eat it like this.' He tucked his left hand behind his back and scooped up some stew with his right.

'I put my hand in the food?' Beth asked.

The sheikh laughed and nodded.

Zane was already tucking in. 'It's pretty good actually. You're not going to be impolite now are you, Beth?'

Rolling her eyes, Beth edged her fingers under a tiny bit of stew. It was hot, sticky and lumpy. Trying not to drop it, she scooped some into her mouth and swallowed. It was unlike anything she'd ever tasted, and very delicious. Far hungrier than she'd realised, she scooped up mouthful after mouthful. Soon her hand was completely covered in meat juice and rice.

She sat back, full, and looked at her hand. Gross! It definitely needed washing. After the sheikh stood to wander among his other guests, she stood to find the washroom.

'Not so fast,' Zane said, leaping up. 'Remember the woman from the market and her tent?' He moved past her and paused by the tent's flaps before raising his greasy hand. He glanced at Beth, then wiped it down the side of the thick fabric. 'This is how I show *my* gratitude!'

Beth shrugged, then did the same. Two fresh greasy streaks resembling blood, stood out on top of others left by previous travellers.

'Bet you wish we hadn't run off in the market now,' said Beth. 'We probably missed a great lunch.'

Zane shrugged as the sheikh approached with a jug of water for them to clean their hands. 'Gratitude is an honourable trait,' he said, acknowledging their gesture.

'Thank you,' they both said without thinking. The lip of the jug, embedded with emeralds touched their outstretched hands as the water splashed out. Beth felt the tingle and green energy at the same time as Zane.

After the sheikh moved away, Zane punched the air. 'Ha! That was a bit of toofa!'

'Too-what?'

'Two-for-one! Look at your hand!'

Sure enough, under the now barely-noticeable webbing, the last of Beth's fingers had turned green. She had a full deck. Scrunching and releasing her hand, she looked again—yes, each finger was green. All five. Now they could find out if five had a special meaning in this world. Would it be enough get them home?

'Two more to go for me,' said Zane.

'Then what?'

'Don't know,' he said, grinning, 'but I guess we'll find out!'

Beth huffed. He sounded like he was having fun. 'This

isn't some grand adventure, you know. All that matters is getting home.'

'Either way, I'm bushed,' Zane said, yawning and gazing at the night sky. 'It's been a huge day, or whatever it was.'

Beth yawned too. Was it only that morning she'd won The Chameleon Chart? Surely Dad would be worried by now—watching the front door waiting for her to walk in, or sitting in her empty room? Her heart squeezed and she folded her arms across it. She couldn't think about that right now, she had to stay focussed.

The sheikh bid them goodnight and, as Beth crawled into the soft warm rugs of her bed, she briefly wondered about Kira—why had *her* thumb turned green? Did she have white wristbands too?

She'd find out tomorrow.

In the meantime, sleep came to her fast and deep.

Z.F. Kingbolt

Chapter 10

'How tough are you, tough guy?' came a child's voice.

Was she dreaming? It couldn't be morning already.

'My father says I'm more grown-up than you!' said another.

The voices were coming from Zane's room across the hall.

Squinting against the light, Beth quickly threw on her robe, splashed water on her face and rushed in to see two young boys prodding and poking Zane.

'Get off me!' Zane complained.

'Ah! I see you have met my youngest sons, Musa and Tariq,' said Sheikh Zidan, appearing in the doorway.

The boys climbed off Zane at once.

'Beth, Zane,' the sheikh said. 'I have a request of you both—a simple one. My boys want to play down at the harbour today, but I want them to learn chess. I hear you are good at the game, Zane, so perhaps there is a way for them to do both?' He gazed at Beth.

'Chess isn't my thing,' Zane moaned.

'No? Then perhaps you could teach them something

else. Beth, I'm sure you will think of a good idea. It is important for them to learn from any strangers passing through, to broaden their minds and experiences.' For a second, Beth thought he winked as he said, 'There's an old saying—the harbour can hold the secret to one's dreams.'

She glanced out the window. The harbour? Her dream was to get home.

'Are you going somewhere?' Zane asked, gesturing at Sheikh Zidan's waist. He was armed with a number of swords.

'Other business awaits, so I bid you farewell. My man will escort you to the harbour. I am grateful you have not refused my request.' And with a short bow, he was gone.

'But I want to go back to sleep.' Zane groaned as the boys began pummelling him again.

'You heard him,' said Beth. 'He's grateful we haven't refused his request. *Grateful*. This is our chance. *Your* chance.'

Zane finally tumbled out of bed, scattering the sheikh's sons who tagged along to breakfast in the courtyard.

Kira was nowhere to be seen although Beth looked and looked, hoping to ask her about her hand. She gulped down her flatbread and honey and then Jumbie arrived, ready to escort them all to the harbour. Beth sighed with one last glance back at the kitchen.

Jumbie's scar twitched the whole way and he kept grumbling to himself. Beth caught the odd phrase. 'Now I will miss the battle. I will never gain esteem in his eyes.'

Beth glanced sideways at Zane who made the crazy

sign around his ear before batting away Musa and Tariq. They giggled and tried to catch his swinging arms again.

They marched through the food market, where hanging baskets of different coloured spices gave off heavy aromas. Mixed together, the fragrances made Beth giddy. She was grateful for the fresh ocean air that greeted her once the street passages spilled onto a curved sandy beach.

At the end of the shore, the five boats she'd seen yesterday were still moored at a wooden dock. They floated in a calm sea, their white sails limp. Many children ran about on the harbour's edge and Musa and Tariq rushed down to greet their friends.

'Snotty nosed kids,' Zane muttered. 'What should we do with them?'

Beth shrugged, rubbing her head. She still felt giddy and didn't know what to do with them either—there were no computers here. 'Tell jokes? But nice jokes! You go ahead. I need to sit here for a minute. I'll be down once my head clears.'

With a huff, Zane sauntered down to the children who leapt up and ran away as if hoping he'd chase them. They shrieked with delight as he attempted to get close. 'Hey! Slow down!'

Beth found a place to sit with a good view of the desert, the sea and the city market, and took several deep breaths. As her giddiness faded, she searched the harbour for what Sheikh Zidan had called the secret to her dreams—a gateway home. Where was it?

Jumbie stood nearby, staring darkly at Zane, then her,

then Zane again. Beth tried to ignore him. Somehow being at the harbour was the solution, she was sure of it. But how?

'Can't catch us, tough guy!' the children called, easily out-running Zane.

He was puffing and panting in no time. Beth laughed, knowing Zane wasn't quite as fit as he believed. She wondered why when he'd spent so much time at survival camps?

The boys had a long rope of animal hair now, which they flicked at Zane like a whip.

'Quit it!' Zane yelled. 'Actually, give me that rope and I'll show you something.'

Warily, the boys handed Zane their rope. He wound it round his clenched fist over and over until it was a large rounded knot, like a ball. Then he removed his hand, secured its ends and kicked it upwards. The children's eyes traced it into the air, amazed, then Zane kicked it away, volleying it over them all. They all ran for it, knocking heads as they did. Tariq fell and when he sat up, he looked dazed.

'You alright?' Zane pulled him up with a quick brush off. When Tariq nodded, Zane bounced the knotted rope from knee to knee, then tossed it to Musa.

'Careful, Zane,' Beth called. 'You might enjoy yourself!'

'Ha! Just something I saw on the interweb.'

Musa suddenly thrust a mini knotted rope into Zane's hands. 'I want you to have this. It's made of camel hair.' Woven in its centre was a small green emerald that shone as Zane touched it. 'Don't forget us.'

'Thanks,' said Zane, and this time Beth actually thought he meant it. Another one of his fingers turned green. One more to go.

'Come!' Tariq called to her. 'We'll show you Father's boat.'

Don't forget us, Musa just said. Did that mean they were about to leave?

She skipped after them, along the harbour's edge.

The sheikh's yacht was moored to the side of the dock. It had emerald-green sails, a smooth wooden deck and five tall oak masts. So much wood! She would have thought that trees were a rarity in this desert world, just like back home.

They climbed the gangplank to see a short stone pillar on board marked with strange engravings. Beth's mouth gaped open.

On top of the pillar was a bronze plaque with two moulded handprints—one left hand and one right hand. The fingers of each print were set with a five-sided emerald. Five fingers, five sides. Beth smiled. This had to be it.

She held up her right hand. Zane's green hand was his left—all except for one finger.

'I think I know what to do,' she said.

'But we haven't got the full set yet.'

Musa and Tariq smiled up at him with their father's green eyes. '*A gem without gratitude is grievous*,' they chimed in unison.

'Right,' said Zane, 'but…'

Tariq thrust out his hand for Zane to shake. 'Thank

you for helping me when I fell over.' On his pinky was a tiny emerald ring.

Zane grinned and took Tariq's hand. 'Thanks for the game.' After they shook hands, Zane held up an entirely emerald hand.

'May peace go with you,' said Musa.

'And with you be peace,' remembered Beth, and she smiled as the two children ran off the boat. She turned to Zane. 'So, like the tent woman said—*an emerald hand begets freedom.*'

'Yeah,' grunted Zane, looking back to the market. 'Freedom.' He sounded sad about it.

'You don't want to go home?'

'Would you if you were me?'

'So you want to stay here like DaveT and Jumbie?' Beth went to gesture at Jumbie but he wasn't on the shore anymore—he was scowling at the end of the gangplank, arms folded.

'You must get off the yacht of Sheikh Zidan.'

'What? But his sons said it was okay,' Beth called out before turning to Zane, 'listen, I need to get home. Please! You want freedom, but it's not here. Remember the beggars?'

Zane watched Jumbie step up the gangplank then looked back at Beth. She had her right hand already pressed in the bronze mould.

His left hand hovered. 'I'm not doing it for you,' he said before slamming his hand down next to hers.

Nothing happened.

A slight breeze rippled the sail above them. Children still ran on the beach. The sea grew a little choppier, but that was all. Zane removed his hand and looked around.

'What are you doing?' Beth cried. 'Put it back on!'

'It didn't do anything.'

Then the boat suddenly rocked so hard that Jumbie stretched his arms out to steady himself.

Zane grabbed the nearest mast and squinted at the sky. The wind had picked up and clouds rolled darkly. Everyone onshore was scampering for cover. Musa and Tariq waved as though everything was okay, before disappearing into the city's markets.

'I think this is supposed to happen!' Beth cried as the waves grew and the boat tipped.

Then the boat rocked so violently that Jumbie toppled over into the sea.

'Jumbie!' Zane yelled as the yacht ripped itself from its mooring.

'He's there!' Beth shouted, pointing to the sodden warrior dragging himself back onto the wooden boards of the dock.

Panting, he stood and watched helplessly as they swiftly drifted away. Rain poured down and their limp sails whipped against the mast so hard Beth thought they would rip. She gripped the pillar as the wind howled past.

'This is it!' she yelled as the shoreline receded even further. 'This is the gateway home!'

'This is crazy!' Zane shouted, right before an enormous wave rose and crashed over the boat. He gasped, completely drenched.

Beth laughed, until an even bigger wave heaved up. 'Hold on!' she screamed.

Water smashed on the deck in an avalanche, knocking Zane over. He slid to the other side of the boat, near the gap where the gangplank had been. Beth's heart thudded as he slipped closer to the mountainous sea.

At the last minute Zane reached out and caught hold of the railing, and when the wave retreated he scrambled back to the pillar and gripped on. He stared at the thin railing where he'd saved himself and, as the dark sea heaved, he shuddered.

Beth tensed herself for the next wave—a gigantic one that hurled itself over them, throwing them both off their feet. They plunged across the deck straight for the gap.

Lightning flashed.

The gap yawned closer.

Bam!

Multiple shards of lightning blinded them as it filled the sky.

The rocking stopped.

Beth and Zane sat up, blinking at the calm sea and pale blue sky. Had the storm blown itself out already? Grey clouds floated far on the horizon. Waves gently lapped the boat around them. The storm had…vanished.

Beth put up her hand to shade her eyes. The harbour was gone too, as well as the desert city. There was no desert anywhere, no children, no house on Daintree Street, nothing.

In every direction there was only ocean.

Chapter 11

Beth gazed across the empty expanse of water. Had they been through a gateway or not? 'Where are we?'

Zane leant back. 'Don't know.' He put his hands behind his head and smiled to himself. 'But we're on a boat. And the sea is calm.'

'Why are you so happy? We're supposed to be going home.'

'No, *you* wanted to go home. *I* wanted another adventure. I guess I won!' He got up and explored the boat. It was no longer a yacht, but a much smaller sailing boat with a single mast. 'The good news is, I know how to sail one of these.'

'Good news?' Beth shook her head. How could he be so insensitive? He *knew* she wanted to go home. Beth watched him for a moment. 'Hey, where are our desert robes?' They were both back in long-sleeve tops and shorts. She patted the material. 'And we're completely dry.'

Zane parted the rips in his top. A scabbed wound still marked his chest, but it had faded. 'How about that.

Maybe when we travel through time and space we can't take things like robes and water from the previous world, they combust or something. But on the plus side, our wounds heal faster than normal?'

'Maybe.' Beth shifted in her seat and the boat rocked as she moved. An old bottle rolled against her feet. As she went to kick it away she noticed something inside. She twisted off the bottle's cap and a scrap of newspaper fell into her hand. In bold type was the word *Resilience*.

Her heart thumped. 'Resilience? What does that mean?'

Zane was poking at his chest. 'Toughness or bouncing back or something like that.'

'Like keep going when the going gets tough?'

'Yep. Like endurance.' Zane stopped fiddling with his top and inspected the boat again.

Beth just stared at the piece of paper. Was it simply old newspaper or a sign? Would they have to endure long tortuous days at sea or was it just some leftover rubbish?

She scanned the horizon. It was the same in every direction. No sign of land at all. 'I just want to go home,' she mumbled to herself.

'Who cares? What do you have waiting back home anyway? Family? Friends? A boyfriend?'

Beth looked out to sea in answer.

Zane scoffed. 'Thought so. This could be fun. Dad took me out on a boat last year.'

'More survival training?'

'Yep. He said learning how to sail the sea is like learning how to sail through life. Everything on that trip was a metaphor! Watch for the wave that has no fear. Big fish eat the little fish. All that and other mindless rubbish. I still have no idea what any of it meant. But I do remember this is the tiller,' he tapped a pole attached to the rudder, 'this is the hull,' he tapped the side of the boat, 'and you have to look out for the boom if we turn in a hurry.'

'It's good your father teaches you anything.'

Zane shrugged. 'The first thing he taught me is how to find land.' Holding the mast, Zane shielded his eyes and scanned the horizon. 'Those clouds—we should head for them.'

'Back into the storm?'

'Clouds form above land.'

'Can't we find a fluffy white one to follow?'

Zane huffed. 'Can you see any fluffy white ones?'

Beth scanned the blue sky. 'No,' she had to admit.

Zane licked his finger and held it up. 'The wind is blowing that way too. Wind generally blows towards land during the day, away from it at night. That's how trade winds work and stuff. And look!' He pointed at a small shape. 'An albatross! It's flying out of the clouds—it must have come from the land.'

Beth watched the bird fly closer and closer. 'Aren't albatrosses supposed to be good luck?' she asked as it finally squawked overhead. It circled the boat, swooping low enough to glare at them, then flew away. Beth swore the bird had green eyes. 'I think we should follow it. I don't like the look of those clouds.'

Zane scowled. 'It's heading out to sea. We need land.'

'I reckon it's flying away from the storm, probably *toward* land. Plus, it had green eyes.'

'So?'

'So that chameleon in the forest had green eyes too.' She paused, realising how ridiculous she sounded.

'Seriously? You want to risk sailing away from land because of some random bird's eye colour? Anyway, I'm the one who knows how to steer the boat, so we're going my way.' He set to work, setting the sail so it filled with the fresh breeze, and steering them straight towards the storm clouds.

Beth scanned the horizon again, but saw no alternative. There was nothing else to aim for and no one to ask where they should go.

'Is anybody out there?' she yelled. The only sound that replied was the splashing of waves against the boat. She sat back again and stared at Zane. He looked content and still.

Was it worse to die, she wondered, by a tribesman's spear or to be lost at sea? Yes, lost—because there was no use pretending, no one knew they were here. They had no food, no water and there was no land in sight. And Zane had them heading into storm clouds.

'Shouldn't we do something about drinking water?'

Zane pursed his lips. 'We'll be at those clouds in no time.'

'What if we get there and there's no land and we're thirsty, I mean really thirsty? You'll wish we had some food. If we had fish, there'd be moisture in their flesh.'

'Yuck, who eats raw fish?'

'Hello, sushi? Well, some sushi. Look, there's the albatross again.' It circled lazily to the left of the boat. 'What's it doing?'

'Probably circling a school of fish.'

'Another military survival tip?'

'No. Common sense.' Zane re-angled the tiller, trying to steer a smoother course through the now choppy waves. 'The storm will probably scare the fish. Yeah, see?' he pointed to the albatross flying toward them again. 'The fish have dived deep, so this fella's heading off too.'

Beth held on to the side of the hull as they sailed into more waves. 'All this bobbing around is making me sick.'

'It didn't bother you in the sheikh's yacht.'

'I had no time to think of it then!' She leaned over the side and watched the whirling foam. It only made her feel worse. 'Can you *please* follow the albatross? It might lead us out of these waves.'

'That doesn't make any sense. Besides, it's disappeared.'

'Oh,' Beth moaned, 'I'm really going to be sick.'

Zane inhaled slowly then leaned over next to her, his face pale. 'Actually, now you've said it, I think I'm going to spew.' He held his stomach for a moment, then dropped the tiller and leant over the side of the boat, vomiting into the ocean.

Beth winced and waved her hand for the tiller, trying to reach it. 'Shouldn't you be used to this?' she motioned at the waves.

'Yeah... I remember now...' Zane panted. 'I hated this last year too!'

He retched again and, as the smell reached her, Beth

gripped the side of the boat and emptied her stomach. Afterwards, she couldn't look at Zane. They were as bad as each other. Instead she leant back in the boat and closed her eyes. That didn't help either, as the boat just kept rocking. She had to sit up.

Wiping his mouth, Zane collapsed back into the boat with deep breaths, his hand pressed to his chest. He winced. He must have rubbed off the scab when he leant over the side.

'Did you spew with your dad too?' Beth asked.

Zane glared at her, then returned to breathing slowly and staring out to sea.

Sighing, Beth leant back and concentrated on breathing. Up and down they went. She felt so ill.

Finally Zane managed to drag himself upright and placed his hand back on the tiller. He steadied the boat and swerved into the wind. Then he looped a rope around the tiller and tied it off. The boat stopped wobbling so much. 'Watch the horizon,' he told her, 'it helps with seasickness.'

'Okay, thanks. Sorry by the way, I didn't mean to upset you before, when I asked if you spewed with your dad too.'

'Who says I'm upset?'

Beth raised an eyebrow.

'Fine, but would you want to go to survival camp with my dad every weekend, constantly get told to toughen up?' Zane smacked his lips then looked at the sky. 'You were right about one thing, I sure could do with some rainwater about now.' He looked around. 'And it's getting dark.'

Beth glanced up. The pale sky was darkening quickly. 'The clouds are still so far away. Do you think we'll be there before dark?'

He smacked his lips again. 'We'll get there.'

'Bet you wish we had some raw fish now.'

Zane gagged. 'Are you trying to make me drop last night's dinner as well?'

As he rubbed his stomach, Beth noticed his wristbands. 'Hey, your circles don't look as bright as before.'

Zane studied a circle on one of his wristbands. 'Maybe it gets brighter in the dark?' Zane puffed out his cheeks as if trying not to be sick again.

'No,' Beth said, looking at her own wrist. 'It's not a full circle anymore. Look, only five segments are lit now.'

'So?'

'I don't know. Just saying.' She rested her head on the hull's cool wooden rim, so brown and shiny with its knots and grains. It reminded her of when Dad used to come home from the tree-farm smelling of pine and eucalyptus. She hoped the memory would comfort her, but it didn't. Up and down they bobbed, up and down. How did people do this for a living, sail on boats? They must be made of tougher stuff than she was.

No, she told herself, remembering the piece of paper from the bottle. She could do this—she could be tough if it meant getting home. She could *endure*.

Slowly the sky darkened into night and the five

segments on each of their wristbands beamed brighter.

'Amazing,' Zane said after a while. He was gazing up, his hand steady on the tiller. 'I used to dream of travelling to the stars, to other worlds, and now I'm doing it. Only...'

'What?'

'I thought it'd be more like seeing huge planets spin past from a spaceship or something. Not just, *pop*, and we're there.'

'You wanted to become an astronaut?'

'Still do, if Ripple doesn't work out of course. It'd be so cool, don't you think—discovering new planets, battling a few aliens...' He trailed off.

Beth tried to find a more comfortable position. 'Only the best athletes get to become space explorers.'

'Nah, technicians get selected too. Besides, I *am* athletic!'

She rolled her eyes. Yes, Zane was tall, but he was pretty unfit considering all that training and marching he was supposed to do every week.

'One day,' he muttered, 'I'll be the best of the best, you wait and see. I could be up among those stars.'

Beth stared up. The night sky was a mass of twinkling stars. She'd never seen so many and couldn't even begin to count them. Compared to the size of the universe, she was but a speck.

Up and down they went.

Zane groaned.

Beth glanced at him. 'Thought you said sailing this boat would be great.'

'That was before I spewed.'

The wind grew stronger and waves pummelled the boat harder. Then the night became even blacker as clouds rolled over the stars. Sea foam heaved over the side.

'I'll pull the line and tack the other way,' Zane called to her.

'What?'

'It's getting worse,' he barked, then clutched his stomach. 'I don't feel well at all.' He lurched over the side again, just as water gushed into the boat as it rolled with the swell. They rose in the air as a huge wave passed underneath, then gravity had them sliding down its other side. 'Hold onto the mast,' Zane shouted as the crack of thunder boomed above.

'I told you not to sail into the storm!' Beth gripped on as the boat rolled and plunged again. 'And no surprise— there's no land!'

'We don't know that yet!' Zane peered into the dark.

Beth didn't bother to argue, she couldn't even if she wanted to—her stomach twisted, her throat stung and her head swam. Seaspray smashed over her face, reviving her a little, though having wet clothes made her shiver when the wind picked up. It blew harder and harder, until it was battering the boat so it tilted dangerously.

Zane struggled against the gale to lower their sail, then hunkered down beside her. 'We just have to sit it out. It probably won't get much worse.'

Almost as soon as he said it, the clouds opened and

rain poured down. There was nowhere to go and nothing to do but sit and shiver as their little boat spun and heaved in the enormous seas.

Hours passed, the rain never easing. Occasionally Zane suggested they empty the water sloshing around in the boat, but scooping it up with their hands and chucking it overboard just made them vomit again. Soon Beth felt there wasn't anything left in her stomach. She'd never been so miserable in her life—wet to the bone, shiver after shiver swept through her body, the taste of bile in her mouth.

Endure! her mind screamed while her body ached.

It was so hard to do in practice.

Zane moaned and leaned over the side again. When he brought himself back up again, his eyes sprung wide. 'A light!' he shouted.

Beth looked to where Zane was pointing, his hand lit by the circle on his wrist. 'You sure it wasn't your hand?'

'No, I definitely saw a light. There's another one!' His voice was weak, but there was excitement there too.

Beth waited, squinting hard. The rain finally eased but she couldn't see anything. Another giant wave rolled under the boat, tipping it high before carrying them down into the trough. Surely waves as big as these were only found in deep ocean? As the boat levelled, though, Beth saw a shadow rippling in the distance, silhouetted by two fluorescent lights. They were near land after all!

'Quick, Zane—what do we do?'

'We sail toward the lights.'

'It is wise to raise the sail in wind like this?'

Zane was already unfurling the sail and tying it steady. He sat lower than before, but his hand held the tiller firmly. 'We need to get there, fast.'

'What if we smash onto rocks and drown? Look, more lights!' She narrowed her eyes. Wait, were the lights gliding *towards* them? 'Is that a boat?'

Zane stared at the lights, then leapt up. 'That's no boat!'

Whoosh.

An enormous fish swam past, its humped back towering over them. Two fluorescent lights dangled from its antennae, two over-sized eyes stared at them and long sabre-teeth stuck up from its lower jaw. Beth screamed.

Another swished past, its lights revealing a cavernous mouth full of jutting teeth. Its spiked fins flicked out to scrape their hull.

'Duck!' Zane cried, as two more long antennae lurched toward them.

Beth plunged into the bottom of the boat, blinded by their brightness, only peeking out again once the brightness had faded.

A school of the gigantic fish heaved toward them. They scratched past the boat and sent them spinning. In places, fine cracks appeared in the hull and water trickled into the boat.

'Get bailing!' Beth yelled. 'Zane! What are they doing?' She pointed to where some fluorescent green lights were swimming in formation, sliding down a wave straight towards them. 'They're going to ram us!'

Antennae flicked out as one giant scaly body after

another scraped past their hull, grinding and jarring. The tiller broke off in Zane's hand. Then one antennae caught on the sail, ripping it off completely. How would they get anywhere now?

'We should have followed the albatross!' Beth yelled.

'Too late!'

More fish surged toward them, this time from all directions. Unless Beth and Zane did something soon, it was going to be a feeding frenzy. This time, their fins ripped through the boat's hull like a knife through paper, their lights flashing and blinding so Beth couldn't see, only feel, the quake of the boat being torn to shreds. There was a loud crack, ocean roared in her ears, then she fell into cold, drowning ocean.

She waited for fish teeth to bite into her, as she was tossed among the waves like driftwood. A brightness swelled in one single intense flash, then the roar of the ocean fell immediately silent.

Thud.

Dripping and panting, she landed on solid rock. Only this rock wasn't being pounded by ocean waves or scoured by overgrown fish. It was dry. It was dark. And there was a strange smell.

Chapter 12

Beth heard Zane before she saw him, coughing and spluttering somewhere nearby. She shone the light from her wrists around, until she found him sitting a few metres away. Behind him, and all around them, was solid rock. It was above them and below them. Water oozed over it and dripped somewhere. Beth sniffed. The air was musty and damp, tinged with something she couldn't quite identify. She shivered in her wet clothes. They'd obviously slipped through another gateway, but why weren't they dry like last time?

'And we're certainly not home yet,' she said, frowning at the circles on her wristbands. 'Oh, there are only four segments left. Is yours the same?'

Zane held up a wrist.

Four segments glowed bright, making Beth blink and shield her eyes. 'I think they're counting down to something. Maybe to us getting home?'

Zane squeezed out his top. 'Maybe.'

'Look, we have to work together if we want to get home.'

Zane sighed and stood, then brushed his hand along a rock wall, walking carefully beside it. 'Instead of always thinking where you want to go, Beth, why not stop to look where you are?'

Beth scrambled up. 'Because the last time I looked there was a giant fish trying to eat me! Have you forgotten about Jumbie and DaveT?'

'What about them?'

'I don't want to end up losing my mind too! Maybe you have already!'

He paused, glared at her for a moment, then carried on exploring.

He was right—that comment probably didn't deserve a reply. She was just so frustrated! Maybe getting through any old gateway wasn't enough? Maybe they had to find a particular kind of gateway? But how were they supposed to know what to look for and where? And what about the segments on their wrists counting down? She couldn't figure it all out by herself.

She looked around as Zane suggested and her eyes adjusted in the faint light from a tiny opening far above. They were in a large cave—deep and dark—and she didn't like it one bit. Mr Zane-Adventure-Is-My-Middle-Name could enjoy this cave if he wanted to, but she still wanted to get home.

'I don't suppose your father ever took you caving?' she asked, hopeful.

'No, but we talked about it. Hey, are you still rocking around like you're on a boat?'

She took a step, expecting to feel woozy. 'No, I'm fine actually. You?'

'I'm fine too. Last time, when I sailed with Dad, the ground rocked for hours afterward.'

'Must be something to do with travelling through the gateway.'

'I wonder how far we've travelled already—we've been in such different places and climates.' He turned and shone his wrist lights in her eyes again.

'Cut that out!'

'Only trying to help,' he said with a laugh. 'There *is* that flash every time. Hey, it's pretty cold down here, isn't it?' He glanced up at the light. 'Must be a mild climate up there.'

Beth turned away. It was awful to think how far away she might be from Dad already. And now she was underground. She gazed up at the thick network of tree roots clinging to the walls, crisscrossing as they tunnelled down. She stepped closer, squinting at the strange jutting angles of huge dangling...sacks?

Seven sacks hung from the roots. Something about their shape made Beth shudder. They looked like large headless bats with wings wrapped around their torsos. She edged backwards and her foot brushed against something soft. She turned and screamed. A mummified body lay on the ground staring back at her. She scrabbled away.

Zane's laughter filled the cave. 'That's the funniest thing I've seen in years!'

Beth's cheeks heated. 'You would've panicked too if you bumped into a dead body.'

Zane moved to examine the sacks overhead. 'Some cultures wrap their dead and leave them in trees so animals can't get them.'

'How come you're such an expert?'

'School project in Year Five.'

Great, now he probably thought her stupid for not knowing. She knelt by the mummy to examine it and prove she wasn't scared, only to hear Zane groan. 'What?'

'Another piece of cryptic advice.'

Beth looked to where he was pointing. From this angle, the shaft of light shone onto a carved panel running along one wall. She read the inscription aloud. '*To see the sun, two steal the sun. Find the nest and work as one.*'

'Steal the sun?' Zane scoffed. 'How are we supposed to do that?'

Beth shook her head. 'We can't. It's probably a metaphor.'

'I hate metaphors, remember.'

'I'd say we don't have to actually steal a sun—it might be the name for something else.'

Zane jumped up, trying to grab a tree root. 'I say it's *not* a metaphor. We might not be able to steal a sun in our world, but we're not there right now. Anything could happen here.'

'True.'

'Let's just get above ground and go from there.'

'Or we could try searching for a nest, because that's what the inscription says: *find the nest.*'

'And how are we supposed to do that down here, in a cave, in the *dark*?' He kicked the rubble around his feet.

Beth shrugged, then shivered again in her sodden clothes. She glanced back at the mummy. Maybe there was a nest beneath it? Or in it? Ew!

Using the glow from her wrists, she crouched down to study it more closely, starting with the transparent wrinkled coating over its face. The wrap extended downwards, thickening into a sack, clear in some places, dense grey in others. The outline of body parts bulged where it thinned. One hand was bent back, its fingers clawing at the coating. She tried pulling some of it away but it was tough as nylon fabric.

Then her breath caught. A band circled the mummy's wrist and there was a name-tag on its chest. 'Zane! Look at this.'

He crouched beside her and peered at the lettering. 'Silwolf. Hmm.'

'Sounds familiar, right?'

'Yeah, another old Tordon player. I played against him a couple of months back.'

'Me too. I hoped I'd remembered wrong.'

'He was one of the best—always online. Then he was just gone.' Zane let out a long hiss between his teeth. 'How did he get here though? Same way we did? Hey,' he stilled for a moment, holding his breath. 'Did you feel that rumbling?'

'What, in the ground?'

Zane nodded and Beth concentrated, unmoving. Yes, there was a faint vibration through her feet. Dust shook from the tree roots above them as something thundered in the distance. A train? The vibration increased until the sacks above them swayed dangerously.

'Watch out!' she cried, running to shelter in a nook nearby. No dead people were going to fall on her today.

Zane ran past her and ducked into a wider hole—only it turned out to be an archway. From the faint glow at his wrists, Beth could make out stairs behind him, rising into blackness.

'Stairs!' she yelled, pointing.

Zane turned to look, then waved her over.

She quickly glanced behind her as the rumbling faded. Was there a way out here too? Maybe once, but it was now half-blocked by fallen rocks. They'd have to climb over and squeeze through the gap at the top. She hurried over to Zane.

'Look,' he said, grabbing an object mounted on the wall, 'here's a torch.' With a whoosh, a burst of dazzling light flamed from the object, instantly outlining mummies, rubble and walls. 'Whoa!' Zane held the burning torch aloft. 'Some sort of motion sensor? I bet civilisation's this way.' He took off up the stairs.

Beth raced to follow before he could leave her in darkness. 'Wait! You have the only torch!' Rubble covered the stone staircase too, having fallen from a cracked ceiling. 'We're supposed to work *as one*, remember?'

Zane leapt over a giant root grown across the steps. As she clambered after him, a breeze chilled her wet clothes again. Where was that wind coming from?

A few steps further and they reached a small landing.

A narrow passage led off to one side—the source of the breeze. Zane continued up the stairs.

'What about this passage?' Beth called from the landing.

'I'd rather get out!' he called back.

'But the nest!'

The ground trembled again and Beth stepped into the side passage, hoping it would hold stronger than the cracked ceiling over the stairway. Signs of recent rock falls were everywhere and it all looked so ancient and crumbling.

The rumblings grew louder, more violent too.

She crouched, shielding her head with her arms.

An ear-splitting explosion cracked through the air and Zane screamed. Rocks tumbled down the stairs, some even hitting her where she huddled, nearly knocking her off her feet. Dust clouding the air made her cough.

Then the quake ceased as abruptly as it began. A few pebbles skittered and settled while Beth coughed and spat dirt, wary of the complete stillness. She checked her arms and legs: bruised, but nothing broken. 'Zane?'

The blackness absorbed her call. No answer.

She groped her way onto the landing, her stomach churning at the thought of him crushed under tonnes of rock. 'Zane?'

Light flickered through swirling dust further up the steps. Then a moan. 'Beth?'

'Zane!' she cried.

A stone slab scraped and shifted, and Zane's head appeared. He slowly scrambled out and clambered down toward her, still bearing the torch which flared again as he moved. She'd never been so glad to see him. 'Are you okay?'

He paused to rub his shoulder and winced. 'I'm black and blue, but fine—considering. You?'

'Good enough.'

With a crunching sound, the rocks behind Zane collapsed further. Beth flinched as he leapt over the last section, landing beside her.

'I guess that way's blocked now?' she asked.

He nodded shakily. 'No civilisation that way.' A large gash ran down his neck.

'Here, let me carry that for a while,' she said, taking the torch. 'You're hurt.'

He felt his neck and surprise crossed his face at the blood on his fingers. 'I've had worse.'

'True,' Beth smiled, remembering his chest. 'Ready?' After waiting for him to nod, she headed through the rubble-free side passage and into a tall oval chamber. Two more passages continued out from its opposite end.

'This place is a labyrinth,' Zane muttered.

As their torchlight danced across the chamber walls, carvings appeared in the rock, seeming to twitch and move as the light flickered. Beth shifted the flame closer to the images, searching for any clue about a nest.

High up were engravings of dragons flying amid a moon and stars; at head height were birds, bats and insects; lower down, three-headed monkeys poked their faces between trees; then a river flowed around giant frogs with long tongues catching fish.

Lowest, on the bottom of the wall, an impossibly long snake coiled through a cave system. It reached from one end of the oval chamber to the other, its scales forming a decorative mural. Screaming men and women were visible through a cut-out section of its stomach.

'Whoever made these,' Zane said, running his hand along the carvings, 'must've worshipped these creatures. Look at the detail.' Each creature had been carved down to the lines of pain on the people's faces. 'Can't see anything about a nest, though.'

'No,' sighed Beth. She switched her attention to the opposite wall.

There, a thick circular slab was carved deep. Rays of rippling lines and triangular segments spread from a central hollow towards the slab's outer edges. It looked like a sun.

'Now we're talking,' Zane said, bracing his hands on each side of the stone slab. He pushed and pushed. It didn't budge.

Beth set the torch down and they each shoved at a side.

Nothing moved except more dust. They tried digging their fingers into the deep crack around the slab and pulling, pressing each ray then pressing them in patterns, then trying to turn the disc around—all with no result.

Zane scratched the back of his head. 'What are we missing?'

Beth passed the torch slowly around the sun. 'It looks like Tordon's Rune of Fire. What if...' She touched the flame to the central hollow and waited. A trickle of dust settled at their feet. 'I guess not.'

Zane narrowed his eyes at the slab. 'Look, is there a piece missing?' He pointed at the hollow. 'Maybe something goes there, like some sort of key?' He paused. 'It's egg-shaped.'

'Which is why we need to find the nest…'

'To get our egg-key for the door!'

'It's big, though, that hollow,' said Beth. The size of a football.

'Yep.'

'Which means the nest we've got to find…'

'…is enormous.' Zane shook his head. 'I'd hate to think what size of creature could make an egg that big!'

'Dinosaurs don't exist anymore, if that's what you're thinking.'

'They don't exist on *our* world. But as I keep saying, we're not in *our* world anymore. Shall we try those two passages over there?' He gestured at the other side of the room. 'Take the left one, then if we come across any other passages, keep turning left so we'll know how to retrace our steps?'

'It's as good a plan as any.' Holding the torch tight, she led the way.

The left passage wound gently down and around, the air growing colder and colder until they had to huddle close over the torch for warmth. They passed two more openings on the right before stopping at an arch with a caved-in ceiling. Beth peered over the fallen rocks where a shaft of light glowed faintly. Her heart sank. They were back where they'd begun—across from the burial cave with the mummies. Only, from this side she could see there was a tunnel between their passage and the burial chamber, crossing through the rockfall. It smelt like vinegar. That must have been the smell she couldn't identify earlier, only it was stronger now.

'Okay,' she said, trying to stay positive. 'Let's go back and try the first passage we find.'

Zane sighed and turned, but stopped as the rumbling returned, sounding like a distant train approaching an underground station. Beth held onto the passage walls, watching the tops of the sacks in the burial cave swaying again. A scraping sound swelled behind the rock pile, as deafening as a thousand knives being sharpened.

'Something's coming!' Zane shouted above the noise.

Beth stared at the tunnel, her eyes widening as a cylindrical body of black scales the size of dinner plates slithered past. She slammed a hand over her mouth to stop herself screaming. It was at least a minute before the last of the scales disappeared.

Zane let out a string of curses before Beth stated the obvious. 'I guess we've just realised whose nest we're supposed to find.'

Z.F. Kingbolt

Chapter 13

Beth gripped the torch tighter as she remembered the mural in the oval chamber—a giant snake that ate people. Great. Going after that snake was the only way to find its nest and their way home, *if* they didn't get eaten.

'We'll have to climb over this rockfall to follow it,' she whispered, shaking the images from her mind. She pulled herself up, the rocky edges scraping her knees. It was surprisingly easy, since there were multiple footholds and handholds. Hearing no sound of movement behind her, she glanced back down to check on Zane and held out the torch to light his way. 'Come on, it's not that high. The forest ridge was higher.'

He shuddered, but began to climb.

After scrambling up and over the top, Beth jumped down into a smooth rounded tunnel. They stood for a moment peering into the blackness.

'Reckon this might've been part of an underground river once,' said Zane, scuffing the floor with his toe. 'Dry as a bone now though.'

'I wish I was dry.' Beth shivered again.

'I wish I had a drink. All this dust is making me thirsty.'

'Now that you mention it,' Beth swallowed, her mouth dry.

The torch flickered, then dimmed.

'I don't think this flame will last much longer.' Beth tried to keep her voice steady.

'Then we'd better hurry,' Zane said, heading off in the wake of the rumbling snake.

Beth leapt after him and they started running, past pillars, around bends, and up and down slight slopes. Occasional broken stalagmites and stalactites were smoothed where the snake must have passed many times. All along the tunnel were small pebbles, though when Beth accidentally kicked one it crumbled apart, releasing a vinegar stench into the air. Was that snake poop?

Trying not to think about it, she kept running until a wall of rock blocked their way. The only way forward was through a dark, low gap at the bottom. There was nowhere else the snake could have gone.

Zane peered under the rock. 'Maybe we missed something?'

'Are you claustrophobic as well?'

'Of course not. What's scary about small spaces?' But his lips were pressed together and he began pacing.

'The snake must have flattened itself to get through, see?' She grabbed a thin black sheet from under the rocks. 'Here's one of its scales. They're everywhere under there.' She shone the torch through, then lay flat and wriggled beneath the rock. 'Come on,' she called back, 'I think I see a way out.'

She finally heard him shuffle after her. The gap was wider than it looked and high enough to pull herself through by her elbows. She refused to think of the tonnes of rock above, or of the torch dimming to an orange glow, making the rocks ahead burn like embers. All that mattered was following that snake. As long as it didn't come back the same way!

Panic tightened her chest at the thought of crawling into a snake's mouth without knowing. Then the rock above abruptly gave way to emptiness.

An unknown light source caused hundreds of stalactites to glow orange in the ceiling of a vast cavern. Below was a lake, the mirrored points of the stalactites glimmering in its surface. It was large, its watery surface spanning the width of the cavern—from a huge rock pile on Beth's left all the way over to a sheer cavern wall on her right. On the opposite shore she could make out several dark openings. There was no way across except by swimming.

'Zane,' she hissed, shining the torch into the gap. 'I'm out.'

'Where's the snake?' he asked before standing up.

'Can't see it.'

He stood beside her and looked around. 'Could be in any one of those.' He pointed at the dark openings across the lake. 'Or in there.' He gestured at the lake itself, although its surface was flat and free of ripples. 'Great, there goes our light.' He took the fading torch from Beth's hand. Coughing, he hurled it into the lake where it splashed and briefly sizzled.

'Don't announce we're here!' she squeaked.

Zane winced. 'Sorry.'

'Shush, I get enough of that at home.' She let her eyes adjust, then looked again at the distant light. It seemed to be coming from behind the rock pile on the left of the lake. 'Perhaps there's another torch over there?'

'Could be.' Zane crouched at the lake's edge and scooped water into his mouth with his hand. 'It's good.'

Beth knelt and drank too, tasting cold limey water while watching the lake for ripples.

Zane finally raised his head and wiped his mouth, eyeing the rock pile. 'You know, if we climb along that rock edge we might not have to get wet again.'

Beth felt water slosh in her belly as she rose and studied the rocks. It might be possible. 'I like the way you think, 007.'

He laughed and clambered onto a long stony shelf at the bottom of the rock pile. Slime coated the shelf's surface, while higher up the rocks it looked dried and easier to navigate, so they climbed higher and continued around.

Massive tree roots, thicker than Beth's waist, draped down from the ceiling too, offering something to grab onto. Once they neared the glow, they hauled themselves even higher and stared across a relatively flat top. The glow was coming from a pit deep inside the middle, a few metres away. They crawled up and over to the pit.

'Whoa, check it out.' Zane pointed down.

The pit was about the height of a room, circular with a dirt floor covered in enormous eggs—so many Beth couldn't count them—and nesting in their centre blazed a fiery orb the size of a football, unbearably bright and completely out of reach.

'Well, great,' Zane said. 'We've found the nest. Now I guess we have to work *as one* to raid it.'

'That's not our only problem. Look.' Individual eggs were shifting, fine cracks tracing their shells. 'Some are hatching. Mum's probably gone looking for something to feed them.' She shuddered as she again remembered the mural in the oval chamber.

Zane glanced sideways at her. 'Well...' He looked away again. 'Nah. You won't like it.'

'What? Why?'

'Because you're gonna have to trust me and I know you won't do that.'

'Just tell me.'

'Okay. So I tie these roots around you, hook them over that one running across this ledge and lower you down. You grab the glowing egg thing, I haul you up, then we're out of here.'

'That's the worst idea I've ever heard. A root will never take my weight. And you don't have the strength to lift me.'

'You got another idea?'

She searched the cavern, then glanced back at Zane who flexed his arm muscles. 'Come on, I've been to survival camp. I can hold you. Trust me!'

She paused, but there really was no other way. 'Okay, I'll do it.'

'You're small and light...'

'I said, I'll do it,' she snapped, already regretting her decision. 'What about your chest?' She gestured at his neck. 'And that cut from the rockfall?'

'I'm fine. I won't drop you, I promise. However much I like adventure, I really want to get out of this one.'

'Okay,' she said suddenly. 'Let's hurry.'

'Great. Grab that, would you?' He pointed to a sharp rock, then started to pull down two vine-like roots from the ceiling. After cutting them with the rock's sharp edge, he twisted them into a rope. 'Arms up,' he said, securing them around her chest and checking the knot was tight. Then he threw the free ends over a thick root crossing the back of the pit, wrapped them around his wrists and tugged.

The harness bit into her ribs.

'Put your full weight on it,' he said.

She took her feet off the rocky ground, steadying herself by holding onto a root overhead. Zane leaned back and pulled, making her jerk forward. The root slipped and splinters dug in under her arms. 'Ouch!'

'You okay?'

Small scratches, but no major damage. 'Yeah. Let's get on with it.' She sat on the pit's edge and slowly lowered herself down until she was hanging by her hands. 'Have you got me?'

'Yes.'

'Right, I'm letting go.'

The harness tightened. Zane braced his feet against a large rock and leaned back, lowering Beth hand over hand. She descended in a series of jerks. With each one, the harness dug further under her arms and made it difficult to breathe.

As she neared the bottom of the pit, the eggs rustled and her ears strained for another sound. Was that a splash in the distance? Didn't it take two snakes to make eggs?

Her toes touched the eggs, their rubbery shells taking some of her weight and helping her to stop swaying. She stretched her fingertips toward the glowing orb. 'Just a bit further!' Another jerk. 'Stop!'

That was definitely a rumble in the distance, like a train—one she did *not* want to catch.

No time to think about that.

She braced her stomach and leant sideways so the roots supported her chest and shoulders. A crack parted an egg not three feet from her nose, sending up a sulphurous smell. A shiny black snake slid out, thick as her arm. It disappeared from view and then cold scales oozed over her ankle. Her heart thudded—why, oh why, was she down here doing this? She held her breath and seized the orb with both hands. It was warm. 'Up! Now, now, now!'

The rope rose, cutting further into her armpits. The coldness oozing over her ankle dropped off.

She pulled her knees to her waist and three jerks had her high above the eggs. The rumbling through the cavern was unmistakable now. The walls of the nest trembled. Eggshells beneath her split. This quake was worse than those before.

Zane cried out, his hold slipping and she plunged back into the pit.

'Zane!'

'Aaah!'

She jolted to a stop, her feet mere centimetres above the cracking eggs as Zane found his hold again. She gripped the rope over her head with one arm and with the other clutched the hot orb. Her sides burned from all the traction. Zane grunted, but she also started to rise again. 'Please don't give up, Zane.'

This time, the nest spun as the rope twisted her round and round. Below, the nest boiled with newborn snakes. There was nothing she could do but squeeze her eyes shut and trust Zane to pull her out.

'Beth!' Zane cried.

She opened her eyes. The top of the pit was within reach now, and beyond it was Zane's face twisted in pain. She threw one arm over the edge, pushed the orb on top and crawled up.

Sweat beaded Zane's forehead as he pulled in the harness. Waves crashed at the edge of the lake. Dirt showered from the ceiling. 'There are two of them,' Zane whispered, helping her out of the root-harness. 'They're fighting. Quick!'

'Thank you for not letting go,' Beth said once she was free, throwing her arms around his neck. She gave him a brief squeeze. His body stiffened, but as she dropped her arms, she spied relief in his face. 'Let's go.' Cradling the orb, she led the way.

In the centre of the lake, two giant snakes were splashing and rolling, throwing their shining black coils as high as the stalactites. As fast as they dared, Beth and

Zane crept around and down the rocks, hurrying to the crawl-through gap while trying to hide the glowing orb from view. Zane went first. But as Beth climbed in, her foot dislodged some pebbles. They rolled down the shore before plopping into the water.

A hiss from the lake vibrated through the air, making Beth's hair stand on end. She glanced back. A giant snake's head reared and two glowing green eyes stared directly at her. In a split second, its body whipped free of the second smaller snake, and raced towards her.

'Go! Go!' Beth yelled to Zane.

She scrabbled through the gap as fast as she could, bruising elbows and knees but still grasping the orb. Zane squeezed through first, then grabbed her hand and hauled her out too.

A mighty thud shook the ground and they started sprinting down the tunnel.

Beth overtook Zane, though she was hardly able to see in the light of the glowing orb.

Rubble skittered underfoot and rocks juddered with the increasing tremors.

Zane yelled and Beth risked a look back—he'd fallen, tripped on the uneven ground. The snake's awful face slithered into view, its emerald eyes locked on its prey. The world seemed to freeze as the monster lunged forward accompanied by the hideous sound of scraping stone.

Terrified, Zane scrabbled to his feet as the snake's jaw yawned above him, gaping five times his size. Two glistening fangs, like metre long stalactites, unfolded.

There was nothing Beth could do except squeeze herself into a tiny space between three stalagmites, thrust the orb and her wrists under her top to hide their light, and peer out.

Zane screamed, his legs and body already in the snake's mouth. With his back to the ground and a rock in one hand, he was pounding the snake's giant snout. It seemed unfazed. Then, so fast Beth almost missed it, its tongue flicked once and Zane vanished.

Silence, but for the thudding of her heart.

That couldn't have just happened. It didn't happen. He wasn't gone.

Beth bit down on her lip, stifling the sobs that wanted to heave from her chest. She waited, motionless, the orb heating her belly. If she moved a single muscle, light from the egg or her wrists might escape.

The snake made a terrible hacking noise, then spat out a slimy round lump. Its snout swayed from side to side, nostrils flaring, then it slithered towards her hiding place, scraping the ground like heavy metal dragging over concrete.

Beth pressed her face against the rock until grit stung her cheek. A cold weight pressed on her back, then slid along her, softer than scales. Its tongue? Had enough dirt and rubble stuck to her damp clothes to fool it?

Eternity passed.

Finally, the creature slid past.

She waited until its scraping faded in the distance, then raced over to the lump.

'Mmmph...mmmph...'

'Zane?'

His fists pushed at the hardening goo uselessly, the coating stretching over his nose and mouth. He couldn't have much air left. She tore at it with her hands, but the goo stretched and wouldn't break. Worse, she could see it whitening already, drying. Soon it would be as tough as the thick wrap on the mummies.

She scoured the tunnel for something, anything. A rock? No, better a piece of broken stalagmite. She hefted one in her hand.

Beneath the goo, Zane nodded frantically.

He stretched the coating clear of his chest and Beth plunged the shard down, striking point-first, then twisting it sideways to make a hole. With both hands, she yanked the shard downwards, tearing and lengthening the rip.

Zane's fingers pushed through and stretched the opening up over his head. He took a big breath and, with the stalagmite again, Beth finally ripped the last bit free of his feet.

Still gasping, he grabbed her arm. 'I bet the snake loops around! It could come back!'

Beth leapt to her feet. 'Quick! We can't be far from that rockfall.'

Zane stumbled up, his eyes wide with fear. Together, they sprinted up the tunnel, searching for the blockage to the oval chamber. The thunder of the snake's approach filled the air again just as they stumbled across it. This time, they both scrambled up and over together, then quickly raced along the passage.

Scales scraped behind them. The creature wouldn't fit through the rockfall, but there could be any number of ways into the chamber.

They got there first.

Beth held the orb before the carving of the sun on the circular slab, its shape precisely matched the hollow in its centre. She met Zane's eyes. Neither of them would have made it this far alone. 'Together?'

He lined his hand up beside hers on the smooth, hot surface and they both pushed the egg into the hole.

Something clicked. The slab gave way and they tumbled forward. There was a brilliant flash, and then they were in daylight—dry, hot daylight that reminded Beth of home. Were they home?

She blinked and looked around.

Chapter 14

Beth waited until her vision cleared and she could see. They were in a vast grassy area, fenced off by a wall so high and flat it was impossible to climb. Glaringly white, the wall shimmered in the midday sun. A familiar scent clung to the breeze, of ocean and fish, and faint sounds of waves crashed on a nearby shore. Birds tweeted. She turned around. The wall surrounded them, forming a giant circle the size of four house blocks, completely trapping them inside. The wall's surface appeared clean and strangely smooth in appearance, unlike the scraggly green trees dotted around the clearing.

Zane stood beside her, rubbing his eyes. The cut on his neck from the rockfall already had a scab. 'At least we're out of the cave.'

'But *still* not home,' Beth sighed, stepping further into the grassed area before them.

Four metal fences interrupted the shining surface of the wall, reaching to the top with bars too narrow to squeeze through, but allowing them a glimpse outside. Coconut palms swayed beyond and further out, an ocean sparkled. Beth spun about to check through the other bars. Ocean sparkled on every side. It looked like they were on an island.

In the centre of the grass stood a number of strange, brightly-coloured structures made of wood, plastic, rubber and metal. Then there was a tiny wooden hut off to one side, some noisy orange parrots, otherwise that was it.

Zane wandered around the wall's perimeter, testing each fence.

'At least it's warm here.' Beth lifted her face to the sun, for once not thinking of its damaging rays. She could feel her clothes drying in an instant. She wasn't the claustrophobic type, but it *was* good to be out of those caves. 'I hope the snake gets its orb back,' she said, closing her eyes.

'Why?'

'It probably needs the heat for its babies.'

'They looked fine to me,' he called from across the grass. 'Besides, it got the orb from the chamber before, right?'

'Suppose.'

'So it will again.' He sighed. 'Looks like there's no way out. Again.'

Beth glanced down at her wrists. Three segments. Surely the last segment would mean home.

She looked across the grass to where Zane was inspecting the strange structures.

'I've seen this type of stuff before,' he said. 'This is an

outdoor playground from the olden days, before the dust storms and things. Looks pretty lame, though a lot less rusty than the ones near us. Dad's never let me anywhere near them, says the government should just tear them down.'

'Sounds familiar.'

'What do you reckon, wanna have a go?'

Beth puffed out her cheeks and followed him towards the objects in the clearing's centre.

The first metal structure made no sense at all. It had steps going up to double their height, then a long narrow slope on the other side that reflected the sun. Next to that was a tyre and three hanging chairs. They looked pointless—one chair even had a chain across the front.

'This is called a slippery-slide or something,' Zane said, rapping his knuckles on the sloped object's metal surface. It made a loud dong sound. Startled, birds flapped into the air, squawking and complaining. 'That's flipping hot.' Zane examined his hand, then glanced up at the retreating birds. 'Maybe we could use this to launch ourselves over the wall?' He snickered at his own suggestion.

Beth rolled her eyes. 'And die trying to fly.' Shading her eyes with her hands, she tried to make sense of her surroundings. It was so hot. She was completely dry now and the slight breeze she'd felt before was gone. The sun beat down on her head from directly above. They were never allowed outside when the sun was this high and they hadn't been able to reapply sunscreen since falling into the ocean. She moved to stand under the shade of a tree and glanced into the leafy palm tops jutting above the fence, unable to shake the feeling someone or something was watching her.

Zane noticed her searching the trees. 'You get that feeling too, huh?'

Beth nodded. 'I can't see anything though.'

'We couldn't see those giant fish before they were on us either. Or that mammoth snake. We couldn't see…'

'Okay, I get it.'

'Hang on. What's that?' Zane pointed at the grass under a tree.

Beth turned, but a movement in the palms on the other side of the wall caught her eye. She spun around. There, high up and holding a coconut, was a small creature with a feline head on a muscular body. It threw back its head in a strange high-pitched yak-yak, then glared at her with green eyes. As Beth stared, it winked and shuffled into the foliage.

'Did you see that?' Beth strained her eyes, but couldn't see where the creature had gone. 'There's definitely something up there.'

'Maybe it's some sort of landmine.'

'Huh? No, more like a cat.'

'I've seen stuff like it in Dad's old military books.'

Beth turned towards him. 'What? I mean up there… Hey, don't!'

Zane was crouching in front of a flat green disc.

'Step back!' She rushed over. 'It's moving!'

The disc was, indeed, twitching. One side lifted on an

invisible puff of air. Then the other side raised higher until the strange object gracefully hovered from the ground. Seconds later a green mist surrounded the disc, which then flipped over and skimmed across the grass, whirring as it travelled.

'Run!' Beth yelled, dashing across the grass and dragging Zane with her. When she glanced back, it was landing a short distance away.

Zane scratched the back of his head. 'Could be a throwing weapon, or some sort of communication device.' He stepped towards it again. 'I don't reckon it's a mine or else movement would trigger it. Whoa, there's writing on it. Can you see?'

Beth leaned forward. 'Um, no.

'Hold on,' Zane grabbed a fallen palm frond and used it to flip the disc. They both read the script.

What can you have anytime, but never hold?

Resting the disc on the ground again, they stared at it for a moment. Beth chewed on a chunk of hair. More inscriptions. Why did all the worlds have one? And who wrote them? Had Kaleski left clues so those following him could find their way out?

Not everyone had…

She sighed and gazed around.

'Phew, it's sure hot here,' Zane mumbled. 'I feel my skin burning.'

Beth searched for some cover and spotted the hut. 'Let's sit there, in the shade while we figure out what to do.'

Zane glanced over. 'I guess it looks safe.'

Z.F. Kingbolt

'We'll soon find out. Come on.'

They made their way across the grass, vigilant and alert. Then after a quick glance around it, they ducked inside the tiny shelter.

'Wow, it's dark in here. Is there a light?' Zane asked.

Beth ran a hand over the smooth hot wood and shook her head. 'My gran used to tell me the sun wasn't so hot when she was young, and kids would play outside all the time, often in small wood houses like this. She said it's what 'playing' was like back then.'

Zane raised his eyebrows. 'But there are no screens or places to charge devices. What's the point in that? Hey, look!'

As Beth's eyes adjusted to the dim light, she noticed them too—the walls of the hut were covered in colourful paintings of a playground like the one outside. They showed dozens of children climbing, sitting and hanging all over it. 'What are they doing?'

'I dunno, but it looks boring, just sitting there.'

Beth peered closer. A black-haired girl was sitting on the hanging chair, laughing. She was staring straight at them and looked extremely familiar. Beth tapped the picture. 'Hey, I know this girl.'

Zane held up a wrist-light to see and his eyes widened. 'Oh, it's, it's…'

'Kira?'

'Yeah, from the sheikh's palace.' Zane leant back with a whistle. 'What does that mean?'

'It means she must have gotten out of here somehow.' She thought for a bit. 'Looks like she might have been

146

sitting on that swing thing before she left?'

'Swing! That's what those hanging chairs are called.' Zane gazed outside, then back at the paintings. 'And that one's a climbing frame.' He pointed at a dome-shaped metal frame with a complicated triangular design. 'Still, I don't see the point when you don't win anything.' He paused. 'Do you still see your gran?'

'My gran?'

'Yeah, is she still around?'

'No, she died years ago. I have some cousins, but we only talk online now. Dad doesn't like to get out much these days.'

'Who does?' Zane flicked a large beetle off his leg then glanced sideways at her. 'I've got no cousins. Only one uncle—Uncle Three-Fingers.'

Beth wrinkled her nose. 'Uncle what?'

Zane smirked. 'Yeah, Uncle Three-Fingers. He used to be a fisherman, back when people did that crazy stuff by hand. On one trip, a big fish bit him and he ended up with only three fingers on his left hand. Snap!' Zane covered his thumb and forefinger and pushed it roughly in Beth's face.

'Stop it!' she shrieked pushing him away.

Zane ignored her. 'And after the fish chomped off his fingers, leaving two jagged bloody stumps, it jumped back in the ocean and gobbled them up! Snap. Snap.' He clapped his hands in her face.

'Yuk, gross. Stop!'

But Zane was grinning widely now. 'Then, after it chomped the fingers, it saw my uncle's big old nose and

147

leapt clean out of the water and ripped it off, leaving two gaping holes on his face! Snap!'

Seeing Zane launch for her nose, Beth squeezed out of the little shelter and sped across the grass, laughing. He was so gross!

With a whoop, Zane gave chase, so she clambered up the steps of the slippery-slide—she knew he hated heights. But once she reached the top, the smooth descent looked too inviting. What would it feel like to slide down it? What the heck—she would!

The wind rushed through her hair as she slipped down, only to land safely at the bottom of the metal.

'That was awesome!' She raced around to climb the steps again. 'You should try it!'

Zane eyed the steps warily.

'Come on! If all the kids in those paintings did it, so can you.'

'You sound like my dad now.'

'Sorry. But seriously, come on—you'll love it.' She was already at the top again, but waited for Zane to climb after her. 'Come on.'

Finally, he started to climb, his knuckles whitening as he clutched every bar tight.

Once he was close, Beth let herself down the slope again. 'Woo hoo!' She leapt up to run around again.

Zane was only just at the top. Unsteadily, he sat on the metal and, gritting his teeth, pushed himself down the slide. He said nothing as he whizzed down, only muttered as he hit the bottom. 'Yeah, okay. That was kinda fun.'

'Watch out, I'm coming down,' Beth yelled, racing up the ladder.

'I'll get your nose if you do!' He waited at the bottom, hands outstretched.

Beth squealed and retreated back down the steps, jumping clean over the last three before sprinting towards a large circular object turning slowly in the breeze. As she jumped on, the weight of her body sped up its movement and Zane ran after her.

'This is called a round-a-bout. You're going to take off!' he laughed. 'Hold on, I think I can make it spin faster!'

'Jump on!'

She looked back to see Zane holding the rails behind her and running as fast as he could round and round. Then with one swift leap he was on board too, and the world whipped past.

Beth laughed at Zane laughing, and at how dizzy she felt. She gasped in the fresh air and felt the sun on her face.

When the spinning finally glided to a stop, she stepped off, so giddy that her legs took her diagonally across to the swings. Zane attempted to follow, but walked like he was on a slant. She laughed again and collapsed onto the grass. Zane did too.

'Why won't the world stop spinning?' The grass felt lovely and cool so she closed her eyes until the spinning feeling faded. When she opened them again, Zane was still grinning widely. She shifted onto her side, wincing at the tree-root burns under her arms, leftover from dangling above the snake's nest.

'Is it your sides?' Zane asked. He plucked at the grass. 'I didn't mean to hurt you.'

'It's okay.' She pushed herself up feeling her side gingerly as she slowly straightened. 'I'm all right.'

'No, you're not! Gotcha!' He pinched her nose.

Beth laughed and felt her whole body relax. This was just what she needed after the ordeals they'd been through, and after everything else in her life. Still, she couldn't let him get away with it, so she poked his shoulder with a finger and leapt up. 'You're dog's buns!' she yelled before running full pelt towards the swings.

'Hey!' Zane leapt after her. 'I just got pummelled by a rockfall, you know!'

Beth slowed. 'Do you think we stand on these swing things, sit or what?' She kicked one, sending it on an erratic course back and forth.

'Kira was sitting,' Zane said, clambering onto the plank. 'Now do that again.'

Beth kicked the back of his seat and he swung forward and back.

'Just push next time. And straighten me up too.'

'Like this?' Beth grasped the swing's long chains until they stilled, then gave Zane an almighty shove. He flew up and back, the chains creaking rhythmically.

'Woo hoo!' he yelled as the wind whipped his words away. 'You try!'

Beth hopped onto the swing beside him and pushed off the ground with her feet, trying to gain the same height and motion as Zane. After several attempts, she found a rhythm and was soon flying. Unlike Zane, who was losing height already. 'Lean back when you go forwards, then tuck your legs up when you go back. Like this.' She demonstrated.

Zane nodded, watching her. 'This is fun!'

Beth grinned and closed her eyes. She felt weightless. With the breeze created by the seat's motion, even the intensity of the sun's heat diminished. Why didn't they have stuff like this back home?

Whack!

Something hit the back of her head.

'Why'd you do that?' she cried out, rubbing her head. She put out her feet to stop swinging.

Zane jumped off his seat. 'What? I did nothing. I was on the seat, remember?' He glanced down to see the green disc by his feet. He picked it up and scanned the surrounding trees.

'Was it the cat-creature?' Beth hopped off her seat and squinted into the palms.

'The what? I can't see anything,' he twisted the disc over in his hand. 'What did it look like?'

'Like a really old monkey-cat thing, only small. It was eating coconuts.'

Zane looked down at his hands. 'And this disc moved by itself earlier, remember?'

'True,' Beth nodded with a last glance at the trees. 'Do you think it's safe?'

He tapped it with his knuckles. 'It's just a piece of plastic. Go stand under that.' He pointed to a nearby tree.

'Why?'

'I want to try something.' Zane raised his eyebrows until she walked over. 'Okay, see if you can catch this.'

'What? Why?'

'I saw something like this on the interweb, years ago. Catch!' He lunged forward, flinging the disc as hard as he could at her.

Screaming, she ducked.

With a snap, it hit the wall behind her, then bounced off and landed at her feet. Zane collapsed into a laughing heap on the grass.

'Two can play that game,' Beth scoffed. She grabbed the disc and threw it hard at Zane, nodding with satisfaction as he dived for it and missed. 'Ha!'

'Right, watch out!' Zane flung the disc back. It whizzed through the air, clipping the leaves of a tree's lower branches. Beth reached up and, in one quick snatch, had the disc in her hand.

'Yes!' she yelled, punching the air. She tossed it and again Zane couldn't catch it. 'Fail!'

'No, you fail.' Spinning around in a complete circle, Zane lifted his leg and deftly flicked the disc underneath. It shot high, traced an arc in the air, and almost bashed Beth in the face.

Deflecting the disc with one hand, she flipped it before catching it in the other.

Zane nodded. 'You're good!'

'I *am* the champion of The Chameleon Chart, you know.' She grinned. 'This is so much fun! Oh, I get it!

What can you have anytime, but never hold? Fun! You can have *fun* anytime, but you can't hold it. Look up there!' She pointed to distract him, then flung the disc at his stomach.

This time, he was quick to block it with his arm, sending it spinning to rest on the ground. 'Ha! You missed.'

They laughed together and Beth thought how it suited Zane to laugh, properly, for a change.

Grinning at each other, it took Beth a moment to realise the air was suddenly still. The rustle of leaves had ceased. The swings slowed and stopped dead, and the round-a-bout halted. The chatters and calls of birds vanished too. Beth knew what was coming next.

For the first time, she sighed with regret as a flash filled her eyes.

Chapter 15

Beth clasped her arms protectively around her body, waiting. The glare of the flash faded and she blinked. When she could see again, there were no walls surrounding her or strange structures, no trees or ocean. Instead, she was standing in the middle of an enormous flooded field, edged in the distance by a steep mountainous jungle—a very brown, burnt-looking jungle. Zane was standing nearby.

'Everything's so still,' she said.

'Hotter as well.'

Beth glanced up. 'I guess that's why. Look.' She pointed at the sky.

Where before there had been only one sun, now there were seven—all rising in the east.

'Whoa, seven suns! That's unreal.'

'Is it?' She glanced at him. 'You're the space guy. Is it possible for a world to have seven suns?'

Zane stood straighter. 'Actually, *most* star systems have multiple suns, rather than just one. Although, *normally* there is one giant sun and the others are smaller.' He shaded his eyes. 'I can't tell with this lot.'

Behind each sun the sky was shaded in pink, peach, tangerine or fiery red, making the low-lying clouds glow. A colony of screeching bats raced across from their jungle roost, gliding on streaks of brilliant colour and multiple shadows. Beth had never seen a more beautiful sunrise. Back home the city's heavy pollution blotted the dawn into uninspiring grey.

Beth sighed and looked around them. In the shallow muddy water of the field, millions of bright green shoots thrust upward. Like a ruthless minefield, they were all plotted equally about a footstep apart. Something rippled between them, heading for their feet.

'Not another snake!' she cried, sloshing aside to let the long black body slither past.

'At least it's normal-sized,' Zane said, batting away a swarm of mosquitoes. 'Probably more scared of us.'

A hot heavy breeze blew past them, carrying the stench of rotten eggs.

'What reeks?' Zane scrunched up his nose.

'I don't know, but we need shade. It's way too hot here.'

'*Stinking* hot,' Zane grumbled. He bent to splash water on his face, then squinted into the distance.

The flooded field stretched for kilometres, dotted by islands of rickety huts. Workers toiled beside their multiple elongated shadows. Here and there, bony buffalo munched on withered yellow shoots and lazily bellowed.

'There's people here,' said Beth. 'Do you think any of them have wristbands?'

'We'll check it out when we get closer,' said Zane. 'I'm starving. Maybe we can ask for some food too, fit for humans,' he added, staring at the grazing animals.

Beth chuckled. 'Actually, we're smack in the middle of a rice paddy.' During a recent history lesson at school, she'd learnt how food used to be grown outdoors. Apparently they used earth, water, manure and photosynthesis before skyscraper greenhouses and tree farms took over. 'That could explain why there are seven suns—you know, because of photosynthesis and stuff?'

'Reckon they'd have salmon sushi anywhere?' Zane asked, wiping sweat from his brow.

'I thought you didn't eat raw fish.'

'Not raw fish straight from the ocean after I've just spewed. The two are very different.'

Beth shook her head and crouched in the water, wetting her clothes to keep herself cool. Giant pink flowers floated on the surface, unfolding their teardrop petals into the size of dinner plates. So pretty. She tried to pick one, but it held tight to the muddy bottom. She let go as an emerald snake swam past, its hood slightly flared and a toad twitching in its jaws. 'Okay, let's get moving,' she said, nodding towards the workers, though the thick muddy water made it hard to walk.

As they trudged across the field, the suns rose rapidly in time with the strident beat of a million crickets. The heat soared to what felt like double anything Beth had ever experienced. Triple. Back home, the schools kept kids inside all day if temperatures tipped above twenty degrees Celsius.

Stay indoors and cover up, Dad would say. *You'll fry in fifteen minutes out there.*

Beth tugged down her too-short sleeves and quickly divided fifteen minutes by seven. Would she burn seven times quicker with this many suns? At least Zane's olive skin would fare better than her freckles.

'This heat sucks!' Zane stooped to grab a leaf the size of an umbrella. As he did, a tattered straw hat floated past with grubby straps trailing behind. He grabbed it and pulled it on, water dripping down his cheeks. He turned to show Beth. 'Whoa, your face is the same colour as your hair! You're changing into an eighth sun!' He slapped the hat on her head. 'You need this more than me.'

She raised her eyebrows in surprise. 'Thanks!'

'Ew! There's spiders on it!' He began smacking the hat.

'What?' Beth whipped it off and examined it thoroughly. Her eyes narrowed at its rim. 'There are no spiders, it's scribbled writing—see? *Confusing arrogance with courage leads to dismay. Your heart knows what it truly craves.*'

Zane rolled his eyes. 'A stupid love poem.'

'I don't think it's a love poem.'

'It talks about hearts.'

'It talks about courage too.'

'Well then, you should be able to figure that one out, given you're a champion and all,' he teased. 'Strange thing to write on a hat.'

'Strange that there's always a message waiting for us after each gateway. Do you think Kaleski left them?'

'He could have come here, I s'pose. Maybe he left them as reminders for himself, like those secret messages you set to remind yourself of passwords?'

'Or he left them behind *for us*?'

Zane shook his head. 'Nah, he couldn't possibly have known we'd follow him here, wherever here is.' He gestured around the field as if it hid a thousand other worlds. 'How'd he know *we* were going to fall through his black doorway?'

Beth resisted correcting him. Fall, pushed—what did it matter now? 'He could have left messages for *any* gamer coming through the gateways. There are plenty of other gamers around.'

'But why would so many people even think to break into his house?'

'Because after I won The Chameleon Chart there was a message above the door of the Golden House of Fame: *only champions dare to enter*.' She shrugged. 'It was like a challenge.'

'So that's why you suggested to meet at his house.' Zane nodded to himself.

Beth shoved the hat back on her head as they walked. 'So, you hate spiders?'

Zane plucked up another leaf umbrella. 'And heights.'

'And small spaces,' Beth reminded him. 'No wonder you didn't enjoy survival camp.'

He didn't answer.

'You said before you never liked it.'

'Yeah.' He looked away. 'I hated it so much I used to hide. Like, actually hide. Dad left me at the camp gate and when I'd have to do heights or small spaces or spiders, I'd run off until everyone had finished. I don't mind exploring, but anything else…'

'Oh.'

'Yeah, I'm not proud of it. It worked fine, though, until Wolk started going too.'

'Right.' That explained a lot. 'Why didn't you just tell your dad how you felt?'

'Why? He wouldn't have listened. He'd just bark more orders and threaten. It nearly killed me.'

Beth poked him in the side. 'You couldn't possibly have faced anything like horned tribesmen, monster fish or overgrown snakes.' She snorted. 'Seriously, itty bitty spiders? Come on!'

Zane flicked her a half-smile and Beth hope that meant he felt better.

'Anyway,' she said, wading ahead, 'talking of phobias—if you could watch out for any disgusting furry water rats or nasty swimming cockroaches around here, that would be great.' She shuddered, searching the pink flowers dotting their path, fully opened as bees worked inside.

Zane splashed her from behind. 'There's one!' he teased.

'Cut it out!' Though the water felt refreshing.

Zane kicked several more shoots, spraying water everywhere. 'Oh, loosen up. After what we've been through, I reckon we could survive anywhere! Perhaps we're meant to have fun again, like in that grassy place?'

For some reason, the idea of having fun here made Beth feel irritated.

'It's too hot for fun,' she said, pulling down the brim of her hat. 'We should save our energy in case there's a real challenge ahead. Like more tribesmen in that jungle or another monster.' She waved her arms about, trying to imitate a Hupuleq. With the seven suns now spaced evenly across the sky, like floodlights on an amphitheatre, her every movement sent a flurry of shadows across the water. She mimed a few more moves before sweat drenched her body.

'What were you saying about saving energy?' asked Zane.

'Right.'

Zane inhaled deeply. 'It really is too hot for fun. Look.'

All around them, rice shoots were wilting and turning yellow. Beth licked cracked lips, wishing for a cold drink or even one of the homemade ice blocks her father froze last summer—the summer he still had his job. She glanced down at the muddy water, thirsty. There was no telling how full of germs it might be, not to mention buffalo poop. 'Is the water getting shallower?' she asked, watching her shins. The water level seemed to be shrinking fast as if let out by a plug.

'I don't know, but it might have something to do with *that*.' Zane pointed up.

Beth squinted out from under her hat. Above them the

seven suns were darting about, exchanging positions and bumping roughly into each other as if wrestling. 'What *are* they doing?'

'They're fighting,' a shy voice spoke behind them, 'trying to chase each other from the sky.'

Beth spun around, recognising the voice—though she couldn't explain how or why she was hearing it. Dressed in a blue sarong and ragged white shirt was…'Kira?'

Chapter 16

———

Beth's eyes widened. The last time she'd seen Kira she was wearing a white robe and baking flatbreads in Sheikh Zidan's desert palace. 'Kira?'

The girl before her bowed her dark head. 'I am pleased to meet you.' Sunlight danced on the metal tips of the quiver of arrows slung over her shoulder. She pulled them off and held them out along with a crossbow. 'You know my name, so one of you must be the warrior we sent for, the warrior who will help us win this fight. Which one of you is the warrior?'

Zane pointed at Beth. 'She is. She's BGwarrior!'

'Kira,' Beth stepped closer, 'it's me Beth, and Zane. We met in Sheikh Zidan's palace, remember?'

Kira straightened and shook her head. 'I have never met you, Beth and Zane, nor have I ever been to a palace. We are but farmers here. Have you come to help?'

'Help with what?' Zane asked.

Kira pointed at the seven suns. 'They are killing our crops. Every day, as soon as we plant new shoots, they shrivel in the heat. Our paddy used to stretch to the jungle, now it's dried to half its size. This harvest is our last hope—my village has no more rice.'

'Haven't the suns always been there?' asked Zane, gazing at the dancing shadows.

Kira shook her head. 'We used to have a single sun for every day of the week. Then the suns started squabbling over who was the most important. Sunday's sun said she made people the happiest, by shining on them during their day of rest. Monday's sun said people wouldn't wake for work without her. Tuesday's sun said it helped dry out the harvest. And so on. One day, they all came out at once, and now they refuse to return to their old ways. They're too proud to back down. They must be defeated or else we will perish.'

'I see. Just a minute, Kira.' Zane grabbed Beth's arm and pulled her aside to whisper. 'Um, this is all a bit ridiculous, don't you think? Worlds can have as many suns and moons as you like, the universe is a big place. But suns don't move around like that. *Ever.* And they certainly don't play chase. They're not alive!'

Beth studied his face for a moment, then shook her head. 'Look, we've been shunted from world to world through I don't know how many gateways now, facing all kinds of beasts with different abilities, and clearly in this world suns play chase. Look at them, they're doing it right now. What's *more* worrying,' she said pulling on some hair to chew, 'is that Kira doesn't recognise us.'

Zane glanced over his shoulder. '*If* that's even her.'

Beth looked back at Kira's sad eyes, which were

staring out over the parched rice field. She felt certain this was Kira from the sheikh's palace. Then again, the marketplace seemed so long ago; the day she won The Chameleon Chart a lifetime ago, somebody else's life... Was she already losing her mind like Jumbie, DaveT and those beggars?

She glanced at her wrists. Yes, there were the white bands, Two segments left of each circle. She hadn't lost her mind yet. 'Kira,' Beth wondered aloud, 'did you always come from here?'

'Of course. That's my family's village over there, Semuik. Few people live there now. Even my parents and three brothers left to search for food. I stayed to help the warrior restore order when they arrived. Then everyone can return.' She drew a long arrow from her quiver and turned to Beth. 'Surely she who has hair the colour of the rising suns is the warrior who will help us?'

'There's something about her I don't trust,' Zane whispered.

'I think we'll have to for now,' Beth whispered back. 'Do you see the next gateway?'

Zane peered around the field and shrugged.

'The suns are cunning,' Kira warned when they turned back to her. 'They know it's impossible to take proper aim. And they know how quickly humans succumb to their heat.' She glanced at Beth's pale skin. Then she twanged her crossbow. 'But if you ambush them at midday, when they align to admire their shadowless rays, we will have a chance. Will you help kill them?'

'Of course,' Beth said, though she still didn't like the idea of killing anything. 'Zane? He's a warrior too,' Beth told Kira.

'I guess,' he mumbled.

'Then you need proper clothes,' said Kira, eyeing Zane's ripped top, 'or else you'll roast alive. I am surprised warriors such as yourselves are not better clothed?'

'We've been fighting some unusual monsters,' Zane explained, 'then came straight here. No time to change.'

Kira bowed her head. 'We are grateful you rushed to our aid. Come,' she gestured, leading them to a nearby work hut.

The hut turned out to be a basic shelter—a crudely thatched roof propped up by four crooked poles. Still, it was a delight to get out of the scorching sun rays. Kira handed them each a thin cotton shirt and sarong, and another straw hat for Zane.

As midday approached, the few paddy workers in the field packed up and paddled away on bamboo rafts. This was no time to be outside, the heat was stifling. Heatwaves rose from the field to make rippling visions in the heated air—the outline of a waterfall, a silver rope, a snake. Beth was truly over snakes, but as she gazed across the field she felt something else—anticipation. Maybe Zane was right, adventures could be great. She'd never experienced this much action in her entire life and it was pretty fun. She felt ready for anything.

'You should practice,' Kira said. She opened a small box in the corner of the hut. 'But first put on this.' She held out a bowl and began smearing thick black grease over her face. 'Smother your hat and under your eyes with this—buffalo fat mixed with mud. It deflects the suns' rays and gives us better aim.'

Beth took a breath. Dad's footie team wore black under their eyes. She was on a team too now. She reached for the grease.

Once they were done Kira prepped the bow, caressing its curved wooden handle, running her fingers over the decorative notches carved above the arrow rest, and checking everything was ready. The bowstring itself was coarse twine and its ends looked thin enough to snap with the slightest pressure.

'Will it fire your arrows high enough?' Beth asked. It was a beautiful bow yet looked so...inadequate.

Kira passed it to her. 'Gently, feel the weight. Now pull it back next to your ear. See? It is flexible, but strong. It may not be as good as other weapons you have used, but it belonged to my grandfather and he was a great warrior. Now you practice.' She reached into her box again and pulled out a long wooden arrow. 'Made from the red mangrove tree,' she said, passing it to Beth. 'You load it on the bow and eye the target like this.' She demonstrated then led them outside the hut. 'You can aim for the corner pole of that hut over there, to your right, see?'

Beth nodded and listened to Kira's instructions on how to hold her arms and aim. When she was ready, she pulled back the bowstring and, with a twang, the arrow shot off. *Way* off.

Zane snorted.

'It'll be your turn in a minute,' she said, coolly.

Kira passed her another arrow so she could try again, and again.

Slowly, her arrows whizzed past the pole closer and closer, until finally her last one hit the mark. 'Woo hoo!'

'Can I have a turn now or what?' Zane asked.

Beth reluctantly passed him the bow. It was fun shooting arrows! She hoped she'd be the one to fire them at the suns—like Kira said, she had the same colour hair!

After Zane's third attempt, though, he became surprisingly good at hitting the target. He passed the bow back to Kira and flexed his fingers. 'What can I say? I'm a natural.'

Beth rolled her eyes and asked Kira for a few more tries. Kira glanced out. 'Three more and then it will be time.'

All three of Beth's arrows hit the target and she grinned smugly as they prepared to leave the hut.

'Enjoying adventures now are we?' Zane asked.

'Yes, but…' she looked away. 'I still need to get home as soon as possible.'

'Of course.'

Beth stepped out into the muddy water and shook her head. Is this how the memory loss started, by enjoying yourself and wanting to stay? Focus—that's what she needed. No matter what peril awaited, no matter what the excitement, her focus had to be getting home.

Kira tilted her hat to study the sky. 'The suns are aligned. Are you ready?' She drew a metal-tipped arrow from her quiver, placed it in her bow and passed it to Beth.

'Me first? No, Kira, it was your grandfather's, you should be the first to try.'

She hung her head. 'In our land only warriors can fight, and I am no warrior.'

'You are to us.'

Kira looked up, her face beaming.

'Farmers fight everyday,' Beth continued, 'against nature, the land, disease. Right, Zane?'

'True enough,' he agreed.

'Thank you, this will be a great honour.' Kira squinted and aimed straight up, pulling the string tight until Beth was certain it would snap. The muscles in Kira's neck bulged, she flexed her fingers, then let go, sending the arrow soaring into the sky.

Kira stumbled backward from the force, though tried to follow the arrow with shielded eyes as it plunged deep into a fiery sun.

Hiss!

The ambushed sun hurtled toward the ground before exploding like an angry dragon and extinguishing into smoky nothingness.

'One down, five to go!' Kira crowed.

Immediately, the other suns scattered, twitching and jerking across the sky to avoid being struck. So much for them staying still like sitting ducks.

Zane passed Kira another arrow. 'Keep up your beginner's luck. Try again.'

Kira smiled, then with a determined look on her face she aimed at a second sun. As it zig-zagged across the sky, she had to blink and squint in the unrelenting glare to track its path. Releasing the arrow, she narrowly missed her target, but somehow felled another sun leaping into its path by mistake.

Boom!

It crashed to the earth and fizzled out in the paddy field.

'My eyes!' cried Kira, rubbing. 'They're stinging from the sun's rays, I can't see any more. She-Who-Has-Hair-The-Colour-Of-The-Sun, please, you must take over now.'

Beth took the bow and a third arrow, accidentally stabbing her palm on its sharp tip. She stifled a cry as blood stained the bow. Ignoring the pain, she quickly crouched on one knee and aimed her weapon.

Burning rays blinded her. She had to look away to regain her sight. Another sun hurled past. She couldn't aim. All she could do was fire and hope. On releasing her arrow, it shot into the sky only to skim the underside of her chosen sun. Like a billiard ball nicked by a cue, it jumped sharply, knocking into a nearby sun. The impact sent it spiralling down from the sky.

Pop!

'I got one!' Beth blinked as tears streamed from her eyes.

'Yep.' Zane patted her back before impatiently grabbing the bow and readying his shot. 'Now I'll show you how a master does it.'

Zane squinted up at a fourth sun, took aim and hit a bullseye.

Shriek!

The sun screeched like a banshee at its own funeral. Lightning-like rays shot from its edges, until eventually it sizzled away. Zane pumped a fist in the air and bowed to an imaginary audience.

'Thank you, Zane,' smiled Kira, her eyesight recovering.

Zane passed her the bow with a sigh. 'Here, it's your village.'

'Thank you.' Kira pointed the weapon eastward. But at the last moment, she pivoted and shot down a sun pausing in the west, believing itself safe.

Crack!

Shards of sunbeam rained down. Her eyes once more blinded, Kira bent down and splashed muddy water in her face, dropping her bow among the yellowing shoots.

Beth and Zane leapt toward it.

'It's my turn!' yelled Beth. 'Kira would want me to take the final shot.'

'But I'm better!' shouted Zane. 'Didn't you see my bullseye?'

They both dived, sloshing about to grab the bow. Beth found it first, and stood triumphantly, only to realise Zane was holding its other end.

'Give it to me,' she said, digging her heels in and pulling backward.

'No. I'm better.'

'But I'm supposed to do it!'

Snap!

The bow cracked in half like a wishbone, leaving the bowstring dangling limply between.

'You've done it now! How will you fix that, Zane?'

'*You've* done it, you mean! Always trying to prove you're better. If you'd just let *me* shoot the final sun, none of this would've happened.'

'Don't forget who beat you at Tordon!'

'Please, stop!' Kira begged, gazing at her broken bow. 'No one is better than another. Pride unbalances the chances of succeeding. It doesn't matter who fires last, as long as the suns are gone. But now...' She reached for the bow.

What were they going to do now? Saddened, Beth remembered the message on the hat.

Confusing arrogance with courage leads to dismay, it had said. *Your heart knows what it truly craves.*

She squinted at the sky, trying to figure it out. The last two suns were glowing hotter and brighter than before, filling the sky. Were they working together to overheat their enemies?

Yes, they were—unlike her and Zane. Kira was right, pride was wrong. Just look where pride had got the suns—fighting all the time. So the opposite was...humility, harmony? Isn't that what her heart truly craved?

'Sorry,' she mumbled. 'The greater good is more important than being the hero. I...I'm not better than you, Zane. I could never have made it through the forest, the ocean, cave, or anything without you.'

'I'm sorry too, I guess. Now give me the bow.'

Beth's mouth dropped open. 'What?'

'So I can mend it, silly!'

She smiled and let him take it. 'How?'

Zane looked around, then tugged up a thick yellow

shoot before wrapping it around the break in the bow. But the shoot wilted and tore and he threw it away in disgust.

The suns' heat bore down and Beth felt as if she was melting. Kira's face drooped in hopelessness. Nothing around here looked strong enough to hold the bow together...apart from Zane. 'What if you hold the bow while I draw back its string?'

'Worth a try,' Zane said, wiping sweat from his eyes.

But when Beth pulled back the string, the bow simply collapsed. 'It's not working,' she panted, sweat pouring down her face. She wiped her brow, flicking away the chin straps from her hat. 'I know—our hat straps! We can tie a stick around the bow as a splint.'

'Or a practice arrow!' said Kira, scrambling back into the hut for her box.

Beth yanked the straps off everyone's hats, then Zane twisted them around two of Kira's practise arrows and the broken bow, tying the straps off with complex marine knots.

'Useful, that military stuff,' Beth teased, pulling her hat over her face again. She was dying in this oven.

Zane gave a short nod. 'Yeah, but the bow's wonky,' he warned.

Beth took a step back to steady herself and trod on something sharp. She glanced down.

Nothing.

Only when she lifted her foot, did the mud ripple. A long green tail flicked up before disappearing.

'Come on, Beth!' cried Zane, holding the bulk of the bow.

She nodded and grabbed the top half, the sheer webbing still coating her hands giving her some grip. Then they leant into each other for balance. Kira stood on Zane's right, drawing back the string while Beth and Zane took turns aiming and positioning the bow. They all squinted hard to aim. This was their final arrow.

Twang! Kira released her grip and the arrow hissed high into the sky. Bored with their attackers' squabbling, the suns had stopped paying attention and didn't even see the arrow coming.

Fizz!

It sunk into the highest sun, which spun like a balloon letting out air. It fell down, down, down until, with a *pfft*, it disappeared.

The surviving sun shuddered, then humbly shrank back to a more normal size. The temperature dropped and dark clouds blew in, growing larger and greyer before bursting over the paddy in a tropical shower. Perfume filled the air as new lotus flowers bloomed.

Throwing off her hat, Beth stuck out her tongue to catch the cool rain. As she stepped forward, her foot throbbed in pain. She lifted it, but couldn't see any blood.

Still it throbbed, aching as if she'd trodden on broken glass. Maybe she needed a better look? 'Zane,' she mumbled, 'I'm going back to the hut.'

But as she went to take another step, her whole leg crumbled, her head reeled and she slumped sideways into the mud.

Chapter 17

⸺

'Beth?' Zane yelled, helping her up from the ground.

'I'm fine,' she said groggily, steadying herself against him. Had she just fainted? 'The heat finally got to me, that's all.'

'You are very red in the face.' Kira cocked her head. 'I know, you need refreshment! I shall take you to my home in Semuik to eat our final grains, for tomorrow will be a bountiful harvest. Come!' She moved to the nearest buffalo, which she quickly harnessed ready for them to ride.

Zane helped Beth on and they were soon riding toward Semuik. Beth's foot felt better now she wasn't standing on it, though she didn't understand why they weren't yet travelling through a gateway. They'd defeated the suns, so why were they still in the rice paddies?

She glanced up at the single remaining sun hanging in the sky like back home. There was nothing to suggest it had ever had a mind of its own, or chased anything. Her head reeled again. Had she just helped shoot six suns from the sky, or not? Something about this place didn't feel right, and not just because she was feeling faint.

Zane's stomach growled loudly. 'Thank goodness we're here.'

Beth looked up. Seven stilted huts with thatched roofs stood on a mound of dirt to one side of a rice paddy. Kira headed to one with a green curtain over its doorway, the cloth's edges dancing in the cool afternoon breeze. Beth waited for the breeze to reach her, but a strange heat seemed to be pulsing up and down her body, making her sweat even more than when the suns were battling in the sky.

'What did you say was for refreshment?' Zane called out to Kira.

'Rice, of course,' Kira said, laughing, 'with spicy catfish and fried lotus root.'

'Um…yum!' Zane replied, trying to sound enthusiastic.

Beth didn't care what they ate, as long as she got off the buffalo. With every sway she thought the ground was going to rise and slap her in the face.

'Hey!' a shout rose behind them.

Dozens of smiling people drifted towards the village on long bamboo rafts.

'They've seen us defeat the suns and are returning home!' cried Kira, jumping off the buffalo and waving. 'Look, there are my parents and brothers!'

Beth swayed backwards as she turned to look.

'Whoa!' Zane jumped down. 'Here, let me help you off, Beth.'

'I need to check my foot,' Beth murmured. 'I stepped on something like an arrowhead or…' She lifted it up, but her vision blurred. 'I can't see, is there a cut?'

'Hold on,' Zane peered closer, smearing mud away from where Beth was pointing.

She clutched her head. So dizzy. Suddenly she was struggling to breathe and she slumped forward over the buffalo.

'Kira!' Zane yelled, still holding Beth's foot. 'Come look at this!'

'What is it?' Beth mumbled, her eyelids feeling heavy. Zane had cleaned mud from her cut, only there wasn't any gash. Instead two deep puncture marks throbbed angrily. 'Is that...?'

Kira took her foot and felt the wound. 'It is the green cobra.' Her voice wobbled.

'Cobra? Aren't they venomous?' Beth was sure she'd learnt that at school.

'Yes, She-Who-Has-Hair-The-Colour-Of-The-Sun. Come, you must get down.'

But the idea of moving sent Beth's head reeling. She closed her eyes and felt hands lowering and scooping her into a ball. Her chest constricted, she couldn't get enough air and her head felt heavy as rock.

'Hurry,' Zane said, his voice close. Was she in his arms?

Then she was lying on something flat and solid. Her stomach churned and movement didn't help, neither did the rocking. Were they on a raft? Water rippled all around her. Bile crept into her throat. 'Zane?'

'I'm here.'

'I'm going to throw up.' Gasping, she rolled onto her side and heaved into the water. Voices shouted. She heard paddling and Kira murmuring. Her skin burned. Were the seven suns back? She peered up at the sky. Three green vultures circled overhead and something roared in the distance. Was that a tiger? Or a tribesman? A Hupuleq?

'She's burning up,' Zane said. 'Stay with me Beth.'

She searched for his face but saw only clouds swimming with monster fish. She curled up and closed her eyes again as pain shot up her leg and took over her body. Surely Witheng mutts were biting her foot while giant spiked snakes slithered up her spine.

Air, she gasped for air.

Then a shadow crossed over her and an angry tribesman thrust his spear deep into her foot, sending a hot pain searing up her leg. She screamed in pain while her foot blew up to the size of a giant sun, burning the tribesman to cinders before combusting into a nest of snakes. They slithered across her chest, up her nostrils and into her ears like a Hupuleq's tentacles. The light flickered like a television screen, and suddenly Beth was on the floor of her lounge room where Dad was watching television, ignoring her muted screams.

'Beth,' he finally said.

'Dad?'

'You should start to feel better soon.'

'Okay.' He seemed so far away. He wasn't even looking at her.

Why wasn't he looking at her? She was right in front of him. She was home.

Someone stroked her forehead. It felt cold, like ice cubes, and the coldness trickled down her body towards her foot. Nothing had ever felt so good. Wait a minute. Ice?

She opened her eyes.

Zane hovered above her, holding a wet cloth to her forehead. As their eyes connected, his lips broke into a smile. She tried to sit up, but Kira pushed her back down and continued to press white petals against her foot.

'What happened?'

'She's awake! You were bitten by the green cobra.' Zane patted her arm. 'We saved you with the petals of a sacred white lotus flower.'

'Thanks.' She shut her eyes again. 'I was having this strange dream.'

'We heard you call out,' Zane said.

'It was just the fever,' Kira told them, weighting the petals on Beth's foot with a large pebble. 'You will be fine by the morning.'

'I was pretty worried, you know,' Zane said as Kira moved off to speak with her family.

'I know.' Beth smiled. 'You need me to defeat creatures like the Hupuleq and overgrown snakes, right?'

Zane nudged her arm. 'Right.'

She sat up too quickly and the world spun again.

Zane held her hand to steady her and pull her upright. The circles on his wrists glowed in the late afternoon light.

She turned his hand to look at it more clearly. 'I wish I knew what these were counting down to—going home, losing our minds, some kind of special event?'

'I'm not sure I want to know anymore,' Zane said. 'I thought you were gone just now.'

'I know how that feels,' Beth said, remembering the snake swallowing Zane in the caves.

They exchanged a look and smiled. Beth had heard near-death experiences could make people appreciate each other. After everything they'd been through, she certainly did. She didn't think of Zane as Mr 007 tough-guy anymore, the kid who'd pushed her through the doorway of an abandoned house. He was more than that now. Was he her friend? She'd never had anyone to share thoughts and feelings with before, not even a mother like most other girls. She tried not to dwell too much on that loss, but with Zane around everything felt less hard. The emptiness filled. Would she still think that way if they went home though? Would he?

Your heart knows what it truly craves, the hat-message had said.

But Beth's heart felt torn. She wanted to go home above all else, yet would she lose Zane if she did? Her heart ached at the thought of him no longer being by her side through every battle and test.

Test?

The word made her think of something that she couldn't quite put her finger on, and before she had the chance to think it through, a flash zipped from their wrists, blinding her again.

Chapter 18

It was dark, really dark. Beth blinked as her pupils dilated, trying to soak up more light. Only the single segment left shining at her wrists and Zane's beside her, lit their faces.

'Are we in a cave again?'

'I think we're in a building. Feels like floorboards.' Zane stomped his heel down. 'Can you see anything?'

'Not really.' She angled a wrist so its light shone around the large room.

'Hang on, there's a light switch.' He flicked it up and down repeatedly. 'Nothing.'

'Shush, I hear something.' Beth closed her eyes, tuning into her other senses. She smelled something electrical, like burning metal. And there was a sound of water or…small feet running? It echoed like they were in an abandoned building. Then someone groaned. 'What was that?'

'I don't know. Let's find out. Here.' Zane's hand reached out and hit her stomach.

'Hey, stop groping.'

'Give me your hand then. Right, this way.' He pulled

her along for a while, then stopped. 'Did you hear that?'

Beth nodded, forgetting he couldn't see her. 'Footsteps, ahead of us?'

Zane started hurrying. 'There's a light too.'

A faded glow seemed to be coming from the end of a long corridor and around a corner. The groaning got louder.

'I really don't like that sound. Let's go back.' Beth tugged on Zane's hand.

He paused. 'Yeah, maybe. Or down that way?' He pointed to another corridor leading right. 'What kind of place *is* this?'

'Forget about where we are—look!' Beth pointed at the corner.

From around it came a dozen pale creatures with gigantic eyes, shuffling and groaning. Luminescent green slime covered them, oozing down their faces and sliding off their chins onto the floor. Something gross dribbled from the corner of one's mouth. Another was munching on something that looked like sausages. Or perhaps it was intestines. Or a finger.

Zane froze beside her. 'What *are* they?'

'Let's not find out!' Beth said, tugging his hand again.

'I think I've seen some of them before.'

'Yeah, in your nightmares, zombies from the nuclear lagoon! Let's go before they try to eat our brains or something.' The glowing faces surged closer. 'Watch out!'

One of the creatures lurched to grab Zane's spare hand and held it up, staring at the glowing circle on his wristband.

'Getitoff getitoff!' Zane shrieked, shaking his arm.

Beth punched its ribs, twice, hard. It groaned and let go.

'Run!' she yelled, grabbing Zane's arm and pulling.

They hurried as fast as they could down the opposite corridor, Beth limping with her sore foot. She could only see a few metres ahead through the darkness, but at least they were moving away.

'Thanks,' Zane puffed. 'That really creeped me out.'

'No worries,' Beth said, busy searching for an exit. There were only more corridors, rough walls and the occasional luminescent graffiti. Had the creatures written it?

'*The man who invented it doesn't want it,*' Zane read aloud, hurrying ahead to read another message. '*The man who bought it doesn't need it.*'

'Very interesting, but let's keep moving,' Beth said, spying another zombie-thing a few metres away. It was bumping into the walls, slowly moving closer, staring at their wrists. 'Go.' She gave Zane a shove as he paused by a third string of words. 'Faster.'

'We need to read it.'

'Move!' She was tired of inscriptions, messages and carvings. They only ever got them out of one world and into another—never home. 'Quick, it's coming!'

Zane ducked to one side. 'In here!' He pulled her into a tiny alcove.

'What are you doing? This is a —'

He clapped his hand over her mouth. 'I think our wrist-lights attract them,' he whispered. 'Hide your bands.

With all that shiny slime in their eyes, they probably have terrible night vision.'

She pushed his hand away. 'Probably? You better hope so!' She hid her wrists anyway. The creature was too close now.

Thankfully it just shuffled past, groaning.

Beth shuddered.

'Did you see that other graffiti?' Zane whispered when it was safe again.

'The man who bought it doesn't need it?'

'No, the third sentence.'

'I saw only two.'

'It can't mean anything good if nobody wants or needs it,' Zane mumbled and stuck his head out of the alcove. 'Okay, it's clear. I want to go back to where we arrived.'

'Why?'

'I smelt something like hot wires back there.'

She remembered the electric smell. 'So?'

'Do you remember smelling that once before, in the Witheng forest?'

'Yes, in DaveT's gateway.'

'Exactly. So we should check it out.'

'What's in here though?' She held a wrist up to the back of the alcove. It was a door. She tried the handle and it opened onto a room full of long wooden boxes. Each one had an octagonal shape at one end. 'Some kind of fancy box factory?'

Zane stepped inside and knocked on a lid. 'They're empty. At least, they sound hollow. Why are they so long, oh...'

'What?'

'They're caskets.'

'As in coffins? Ew.'

'Look at this one though.' Zane touched a black coffin beside them. 'Looks a bit like the Black-Door-With-No-Doorknob. There's even a rune on the lid! Tordon's four-rods Rune of Death. Wait, I think that graffiti has something to do with coffins.'

Beth was already backing away. 'The man who invented coffins doesn't want it, and the guy who bought it isn't buying it for himself… Yeah, I'd say the graffiti has something to do with coffins. It's probably where they all sleep! Like vampires!'

'Or it could be our way out.'

'What?' Beth tried to think through her rising panic. 'How?'

'Because the lids look like doors. See?' He shone a wrist over the black coffin, which did kind of look like a door. 'Let's get in one.'

'I am *not* getting inside a coffin!' Her stomach clenched at the thought. 'Didn't you say there was a third sentence? It might say: whatever you do, don't climb inside a zombie's coffin.'

'Fine,' Zane sighed. 'We'll find it on our way back.'

'Great, let's go.' Beth firmly closed the door behind them and hobbled after Zane, who was scanning the walls.

'Here's the third sentence,' he said. '*The man who needs it doesn't know it.*' He glanced at her. 'Well, a dead man doesn't know he needs a coffin, right? Maybe zombies and vampires don't need coffins, but we do? That one *was* shaped like the Tordon door.'

'What about that smell? Let's check that out first…'

Zane shook his head but followed her, sniffing and hurrying down the corridor before turning left round a corner. Soon they were back near the broken light switch.

'There it is again,' said Beth in satisfaction. 'Like electrical burning. And it's coming from those stairs.' She peered into the darkness. 'Wait, there's one set going up; one going down. Which way?'

Zane sniffed. 'The smell could be coming from either direction, but there's more light coming from downstairs. Or is that…argh, not more zombies! Up, up!'

Seven bug-eyed, glowing creatures shuffled up the stairs towards them.

'Quick!' Beth yanked Zane by his top, hobbling up the steps. There was a landing to turn before the stairs continued up, ending in a corridor exactly the same as below, covered in the same luminescent graffiti.

The man who invented it doesn't want it.

The man who bought it doesn't need it.

The man who needs it doesn't know it.

'Keep moving!' Beth yelled.

Pulling each other along, they raced down the corridor. 'This way!' yelled Zane, grabbing Beth's hand and jerking her left down a hallway as more zombie-things came at them from the corridor on the right.

Beth glanced behind her. 'Do you have a plan? Because now there are two groups after us!' Zane turned another corner and she slammed into his back. 'Keep running!'

'Dead end.'

'What?' Beth flicked her hand, using the final lit segment for illumination. An unfinished brick wall had been hurriedly slapped up in the middle of the corridor, blocking them from going further. A neat sign was imprinted in the middle: 'Memorial Hospital— Burns Ward'. Below that was another hastily-hung sign: 'Danger—Hospital shut down—Virus X10.23. Keep out!'

But they couldn't keep out—they were trapped inside, and the groaning and shuffling of virus-victims was getting louder and louder. If Beth and Zane stayed where they were, they'd get infected too.

Yet there was no way out.

Chapter 19

'Can we get past this wall somehow?' Beth asked, trying to hide her wrists at the same time as feeling the wall and bricks for gaps. 'There's a ten centimetre gap on this side. What about your side?'

'Same.'

Beth looked up. 'You're taller than me. Can you feel the top? Can we go over?'

Zane squatted and slapped his shoulders. 'Climb on.'

'Are you nuts?'

'You want to see if there's a top, right?' He slapped his shoulders again. 'Make it quick. See how light it's getting? They're almost here.'

Beth gritted her teeth and trod on one of Zane's shoulders. Her foot still hurt from the cobra bite. 'Don't drop me, okay?'

'Did I drop you over the snake nest? Just be thankful you're not still in a sarong.'

'True.' They were back in their long-sleeved tops and shorts. Beth wanted to think more about that, except

Zane kept wobbling. 'Try not to move around so much, my foot's still sore.'

Zane grunted and gripped her shins, then slowly stood, stretching to his full height. 'Okay, can you feel an edge?'

Beth strained upwards, her hands balancing against the wall. 'I don't feel anyth…hold on.'

'Hurry!'

'Yes, there's a hole. It's big enough.' She leaned closer. 'But how are we both going to get up?'

'We'll help each other.'

Beth glanced down. Zane was becoming more visible in the glowing light appearing around the corner. 'I'm not strong enough to pull you up.'

'Just you get up there first.' He adjusted his hands so they were under her feet. 'When I say jump, I'll push you up. Then reach a hand down for me. I'll just use it for leverage and pull myself up. Ha, now that *is* something I learnt from survival camp.' There was a strange tone in his voice that Beth couldn't identify. 'Ready? Jump, NOW!' He pushed and she launched herself up.

She hooked her elbows over the hole then hauled her leg over the top. 'Okay, I'm up. The other side has an old lightbulb, it's turned on. I can see! There are more stairs and some stretcher things on wheels.' She swallowed. 'I think there's a dead body on one! Ew!'

'Lower your arm!' Zane yelled.

Beth looked back to see creatures shuffling into view. They were only a few metres away. 'Where are you going?'

Zane was jogging over to them. 'I need a run-up. Get ready for a tug on your arm!'

She stretched her arm downward, turning her wrist so he could see the light.

Then he ran at the wall in full sprint.

She braced herself as he leapt and yanked on her arm before scrabbling against the wall. The sheer webbing on his fingers pulled against her skin but he couldn't get a grip on the wall itself and with a yell, he crashed down, landing hard on his side. 'Zane!'

'Man, that hurt,' he groaned. He pushed himself to his feet, checked his neck gash and rubbed his old chest wound. The movement seemed to make the luminous virus-victims shuffle faster, almost excited.

'Try again, Zane!' She stretched her hand further. 'Come on!'

'I can't! You go! Find the coffin room—it's the only way out!' He had his back to the wall as the creatures moved in.

'I'm not leaving you!'

'You don't have a choice!'

A dozen glowing-faces leered toward Zane, their arms outstretched. One at the front had its emerald-green eyes locked on Zane, its luminescent slime twitching as it winked, a jagged smile stretching across its dripping face.

'Go, Beth! I'll fight my way through! Trust me!' He began punching and kicking and she could hear his fists connect with their oozing flesh. 'Meet me at the coffins! Get out if you can!'

Beth whimpered as Zane was lost among the bodies. Maybe she could find something to help fight them off?

'Aaahh!' Zane burst from the jumble, his arms flailing. The creatures fell aside as he leapt off down the hall, though they soon stumbled up to follow him. At least he was running away from them now, heading for the coffin room himself.

'Keep moving, Bethlyn,' she told herself.

She turned and lowered herself onto a stretcher on the other side of the wall. She did not want to be here alone—of all the places they'd been, not here. She climbed off the stretcher and headed for the stairs she'd seen from the top of the wall.

Above the stairwell was a sign—down was 'Morgue', while up was 'Canteen'. She saw more biohazard stickers slapped about too. She shuddered, then headed down the stairs.

A glow appeared from overhead. Was that daylight? No, a pale white hand appeared on the railing above her.

She ran down the stairs, pausing at the bottom. It was the same room as before—the one with coffins everywhere, only this time she'd entered from a different direction. Now where was the one with the rune? And where was Zane?

A groan sounded behind her, sending her rushing across the room. A creaking noise cut through the gloom on her left—the lid of a coffin slowly opening. A drooling virus-victim sat up, then clambered over the edge, keeping its green eyes fixed on her.

'Zane!' she screamed, hoping he'd hear her somewhere.

No answer.

She backed away, only to see the same thing playing out on the other side of the room—another luminous virus-victim climbing out of a coffin. More coffins opened, their lids rising. Where was that black coffin? Wasn't it by the door they'd opened earlier? She ran across.

Yes, there it was.

She opened its lid and got ready to jump in, as soon as Zane burst into the room. Black velvet lined the coffin's insides, making it look soft and comfortable. Still, she wasn't going to get in by herself. She might get trapped! What if she turned into a glowing virus-victim? What if she forgot who she was, or Zane?

Where was he? Why wasn't he here already? He hadn't sacrificed himself so she could get away, had he?

The virus-victims moved in, closer and closer—their arms outstretched, reaching, oozing.

The door opened.

'Zane!' she called out.

It wasn't him. It was more virus-victims, scores of them. She was totally surrounded and if she didn't get in soon, they'd get her.

'Zane!' she cried one last time.

Nothing.

She had no choice. She rolled into the black box and slammed the lid shut. Glowing fingers slid under, trying to lift it and she jabbed each one hard until it let go. There was a light behind her head, so she twisted around to poke it, but it wasn't zombie-fingers, it was a familiar shape. A raised skull with three holes—Tordon's Rune of Self-Belief.

Not knowing what else to do, she reached up and pushed it. There was some resistance, then a click.

For a second nothing happened.

Then a bright flash blinded her and the bottom of the coffin fell away.

She fell through a dark nothingness, feeling her heart break—after everything they'd been through, after everything they'd shared…she had left Zane behind.

Chapter 20

⟶

Beth's feeling of weightlessness ended with a soft landing in a dimly lit room.

She blinked as her eyes adjusted. She was still lying down, but now she was cradled in a white leather recliner. Shuffling sounds made her stiffen, her heart drumming. Was it virus-victims again? A metallic smell tickled her nose and she heard a tiny snore.

On another recliner slept a boy, tossing about in his sleep and, for a moment, her breath stopped—had Zane made it after all? No, it wasn't him. Her heart squeezed as she remembered. She glanced around to see a white room with six others, all sleeping soundly, all roughly her age. She stifled a yawn and stretched, feeling as if she hadn't moved in weeks. Had she been asleep as well?

'Alert!' a siren blared, rousing the others. 'Approaching alien vessel!' From a corner of the room, a green light flashed.

She sat up and tried to get the attention of the boy near her. 'What's going on?'

Before he could answer, an automatic door slid open and a tall man wearing some sort of spacesuit strode in, his chest decorated in medals. 'Attention!' he barked, cracking his knuckles one by one. 'I want you suited up. Tock-rifles on the right.' He gestured at a wall stacked with weapons. The others scrambled to their feet and started pulling on grey overalls. 'Move it, move it! You there!' he strode over to Beth, grabbing a rifle on his way. 'I understand you've not been briefed yet?'

She nodded.

'When I ask you a question, soldier, you say 'yes, sir'. Got it? As captain of this mission, Captain Lang to you, I expect full cooperation, so when I say move, you move!' He slammed the rifle into her chest. 'Now suit up! There's not much time.'

Time?

Beth glanced at her wrists as she grabbed a suit nearby. The last of her segments had gone out...and she still wasn't home. Is this what the segments had been counting down to all along?

She frowned, dropping the rifle by her side.

'Pick up your gun, soldier,' Captain Lang ordered her. 'This is no time for breakdowns. I thought you were the best of the best!' At Beth's blank stare, he muttered something under his breath, then, 'Right, listen up! I don't have time for details, but you've all been selected as the best young people we have on Earth—the best athletes, up-and-coming scientists, pilots, thinkers and doers, even,' he flapped a hand at her, 'the best gamers.

I understand some of you were tested without your knowledge...'

Tested?

'...but that was to get you where you needed to be—here on my shuttle. Remember recruits,' he peered around the room, 'remember that no matter where you're from, no matter how you got here, you're my soldiers now.' He slapped his hands behind his back and began to pace.

'As we've been travelling out here over the last few weeks,' he continued, 'you've all been rigorously tested in your ability to adapt and survive. You've learnt compassion and consideration, respect for other cultures and the value of life. You now know how to fight to survive as well as how to overcome phobias, solve puzzles and work as a team. Of course, some of you left your teammates behind,' he paused to glare at her, 'but that cannot be helped now. Earth needs you. Your families need you—your parents, brothers, sisters and friends. All of them know your whereabouts and have agreed to your testing via simulations developed by the famous computer whiz, Aaron Kaleski.'

Beth's mouth dropped open. She knew it! All the worlds she'd visited with Zane had been simulated tests! She knew there'd been something strange about all those messages appearing after every gateway. Gateway? They hadn't even been travelling to other worlds—they'd been in a virtual selection process. Suns didn't have minds of their own to chase each other in the sky. Giant fish and snakes didn't exist. She knew there was a reason for all the challenges and the glowing segments on her wrists. It was all to get her here! But where was 'here' exactly?

She chewed on her hair, glancing at the others as the captain continued to speak. They all had wristbands with a circle of unlit segments too.

'So now,' Captain Lang continued, 'you must forget any fears you may have, any doubts in your abilities, and focus on why you're here—to save Earth. We're leaving Neptune Base Station now,' he gestured to a viewing port, 'and will soon face Earth's greatest threat.'

Beth gasped as she followed the others over to the port—she was in space! Guilt washed over her. This was Zane's dream, he'd always wanted to soar among the stars, be an astronaut.

It'd be so cool, he said on the boat, *discovering new planets, battling a few aliens…*

Now the dense blue clouds of the giant planet Neptune swirled above her head, while one of its moons, a small orange one, circled closer. Her wide eyes on the view port, she climbed into her grey overalls, leaning back on a recliner to aid her sore foot. It still hurt.

Out another viewing port, the rings of a nearby space station grew smaller. She remembered from news reports back home that the International Neptune Base Station was studying the Kuiper Belt—a stretch of fragmented rocks that orbited their whole solar system. They were trying to find a way to bypass it and eventually explore interstellar space.

Is this where Kaleski had gone, not to Ripple headquarters in India but to Neptune Base? In a way, that would make sense. It was just like the rumours had said, he'd discovered a gateway to other worlds—the planets of our outer solar system.

She swallowed hard as she zipped up her suit, wondering why Earth was in so much danger.

'Now you're all finally ready,' the captain pointed to a spot in the sky, 'this is what we are here to defeat—the biggest threat our world has ever seen.'

Everyone crowded closer to the window. They were approaching an enormous black egg-shaped rock hovering darkly between the orange moon and Neptune's giant blue face. Its near-perfect symmetry and smooth surface looked like nothing Beth had ever seen.

'What is it?' she asked.

The captain cracked his knuckles again. 'We believe it to be an aggressive alien weapon.' He strode to a platform in the centre of the room and lifted a clear box on its top. Inside was a small chunk of black crystal, shiny as glass and as sharp as a cluster of stalactites. 'Seven months ago we discovered this crystal within the Kuiper Belt, and when we cracked it open we found this stone.' He pulled the crystal apart to reveal a bright green stone. Immediately the room lit up from the many circular patterns and symbols carved on its surface. The captain's face glowed an eerie green from the light. 'This stone shone as though it were transmitting a signal across space and, sure enough, within days that giant black problem arrived. We calculate it is waiting for its creators to arrive before attacking Earth.'

'So what's our mission, sir?' someone asked eagerly.

Captain Lang caressed the stone in his hands. 'We must protect Earth at all costs. Our probes have discovered multiple passageways inside the weapon, many large web-like structures with the same patterns and symbols as reflected on the walls around you now, yet no life-forms. And every person we have sent to explore it has failed to return.'

They all gazed out at the dark rock.

'Master code-breakers translated these symbols,' the captain continued. 'And the essence of it is this...' He pulled a piece of paper from his pocket and read:

From the start of evolution,
To the end of time and space,
The start of earthly equinox,
Points to the end of base.

'The end of Neptune Base Station?' cried a blonde-haired girl.

'We think so.' The captain nodded grimly. 'There was also mention of a young warrior, a great champion of a certain age, who could make use of 'the cocoon'—we presume by that they mean their weapon. You're all the best in your fields. It is you who must now risk your lives to save others—your loved ones and family. Are you ready, soldiers?'

The others straightened and saluted the captain. 'Ready, sir!'

Beth followed them. She had to—if Earth was

depending on them, that meant Dad was too. She couldn't stop to think about Zane or getting home anymore—she had to save home. She had to think about this stone and the cocoon.

'Good.' Captain Lang closed the stone back inside its crystal casing, then put it in the clear box on the platform. 'We dock at the cocoon in three minutes and sixteen seconds. Present arms,' he barked, marching over to the nearest soldier to check his rifle.

Beth waited by the platform, gazing thoughtfully through the clear box to the crystal inside. Now she was here, it made perfect sense that she'd been given a riddle to solve at the start of every gateway. Gateway, or level? Whichever way she looked at it, this little green stone held the most important riddle of all. Shouldn't they take it with them when they docked, in case they needed it once exploring the cocoon?

Of course, if they were supposed to take the stone, surely someone would have suggested it already?

She bit her lip, thinking about the last thing she'd seen before arriving here, on the inside of that virus-victim coffin—a raised skull with three holes, Tordon's Rune of Self-Belief. They should take the stone. Something was telling her to take the stone.

So, while everyone was busy with their weapons, she quickly lifted the box's lid and with trembling fingers swiped the black crystal. She slid it inside the pouch she'd noticed on her suit. Her heart beating madly, she checked no one had seen her. No, they were all still gazing outside, watching other shuttles dock at strategic positions around the giant cocoon. Were they the best of the best too?

Beth shook her head. It didn't matter how many teams were helping—only that they solved their common goal, quickly and effectively. Kira from the rice paddies had taught her that much. She turned her thoughts to the message.

The start of evolution could be 'life', and the end of time and space...'nothing'? An equinox meant *equal* day and night times, so 'life equals nothing'?

Beth narrowed her eyes in thought. It couldn't be that. And what of the warrior?

Then she laughed to herself, BGwarrior. If anyone was a warrior around here, it was her...and yet she'd stolen the stone. It burned in her pouch almost as much as her cheeks, but somehow she sensed they would need it.

'Back to your seats, soldiers!' the captain ordered. 'We're about to dock!'

Beth scrambled back to her recliner as a rumble grew to a roar from the engines gearing to land. Then there was a jolt and they were still.

The captain stood by the door of their shuttle. 'Helmets on! It's time.'

Chapter 21

Beth quickly donned her helmet, checked her torch and passed a comms test to make sure she could hear and speak with the others. Then the shuttle door opened.

She felt like an ant about to enter a mountain. A miserable ant. If only Zane were with her. His absence felt all the more stark when the other six recruits filed up to enter the cocoon—in groups of two.

Beth took a deep breath and tried not to think about it. What did her feelings matter when so many people were relying on her, when Dad was relying on her, Zane too? If she and Zane had been doing all that testing while sleeping in stasis as they travelled to Neptune, he was probably back at the Space Station somewhere.

Beth shuddered to think he might still be fending off virus-victims in his sleep. What a nightmare. Surely they'd have switched his simulation off by now? He may not have passed the final test, but just being in space would make up for everything, she was sure.

'Forward, march!' yelled the captain, and they shuffled into a dark cavity with a low-ceiling and hard uneven floor. Why was the cocoon even allowing shuttles to come and go?

She gripped her torch tighter. The other recruits had their rifles at the ready, but hers was slung over a shoulder.

Every person we have sent to explore it, the captain had said of the cocoon, *has failed to return.*

Beth was determined to do something different from the others, do things they hadn't done, ask what they hadn't asked, see what they couldn't see...Her eyes widened, trying to take in everything around her, and she almost tripped on the uneven surface underfoot. She lifted her sore foot and marvelled that she didn't float away. Was gravity magnetised to their boots somehow? However created, it meant they were able to walk normally, which was great because all around them were the same swirly patterns as on the crystal's green stone, only these weren't glowing. The cave was covered with them, as were three passageways leading away into darkness.

'Soldiers!' Captain Lang barked through their comms. 'Look around and holler if you find anything. We may need to split up if we're to search this place thoroughly. Choose a passage.'

Beth knelt and examined the swirls on the ground, then shone her torch on the walls. The patterns were tiny black crystal carvings, only in different shades—onyx, charcoal and jet. One of the patterns looked very familiar. What was it?

The start of evolution, she repeated in her mind, *the start of evolution, what starts evolution...?*

Then she got it! Like the rhyme said, at the start of the *word* evolution was the letter 'e', and the *words* time and space ended with an 'e' too. The words earthly and equinox also started with the letter 'e', and the word base ended in an 'e' as well.

She traced the nearest 'e' swirl with her finger, the familiar pattern she'd recognised.

Could it be that simple?

She glanced around and saw the pattern above the right-hand passage, but not the other two. Perhaps it indicated the correct passage to take? She had to tell the captain! But as she went to speak up, the thud of boots vibrated on the ground and a familiar voice burst through her comms unit.

'Captain, sir!' he said. 'Corporal Ed and team approaching, sir! We've come from shuttle twelve and there's a screaming vibration coming this way! We've been sent to warn you!'

As the others began babbling in panic, Beth gasped. She'd know that voice anywhere!

'Zane!' she shouted and limped forward, just as he burst from the far left tunnel with a group of others, all armed. His face had that familiar hard look she remembered from Daintree Street, stubborn and closed. He didn't look like the boy she'd come to know at all. 'Zane?'

Not answering her, he dashed over to salute the captain. 'Captain, we should get these civilians out of here!'

'Zane?' she called through the comms, waving her arms. 'Remember me? It's Beth!'

He turned to look at her, his expression blank. He didn't know who she was!

'Corporal,' Captain Lang asked, 'do you know this girl?'

'No, sir.'

'Then eyes to me, soldier. How close is this vibration?'

'I'd say two minutes, sir. We must fall back.'

Beth glanced behind her, but the shuttle had already gone. It had left them here?

'With your permission, sir?' yelled Zane, gesturing with his rifle down the middle passage.

'Granted,' agreed the captain.

'Everyone,' Zane yelled to the recruits, 'run!' Then he spun on his heels and began jogging away. The wrong way. The rest of his team followed.

'Recruits!' barked the captain, sweeping his arms wide. 'You heard the man, move out! Move it, move it.'

'Zane!' Beth screamed, sprinting as best she could with her sore foot until she'd overtaken his team and caught his arm, yanking him back. 'Wait! You're...'

But before she could finish, he knocked her sideways with the butt of his rifle. 'Just run!'

She gasped. The Zane she had come to know would never have done that. That Zane was her friend—one she had earnt through hard times as well as fun. Where had those times gone now? She froze and stared at him.

'It's no time for goggling at boyfriends, soldier!'

shouted the captain, heaving her to her feet as the others thundered past. 'Get moving!'

'But it's the wrong way!' shouted Beth. 'It's the other tunnel—I solved the puzzle!'

'What?' Zane stopped, as did everyone else. The tunnel was crowded as everyone tried to turn about and look at her.

'We have to go back!' Beth cried.

'We can't go back!' yelled the captain. 'Look!'

A high-pitched humming vibrated from the tunnel. It grew so loud they felt it pinging in the back of their heads. Then a pale light appeared and strengthened as they all turned to look. It became whiter and whiter until an enormous pale worm emerged. It erupted into the tunnel with a mighty screech.

Someone fired their rifle at it, but the bullets just bounced off the creature with a plink.

Screaming broke out as everybody scrambled to get away.

'I don't understand,' cried Captain Lang, 'our probes detected no life-forms!'

'It called itself a cocoon, right?' yelled Beth, racing after Zane. She was determined to keep him in sight. 'So there's your grub! It must have been in hibernation!'

The passage twisted and turned, and rocks were strewn about. No wonder this mission needed soldiers experienced with dark cave systems. 'Nothing new for me,' she panted. Or Zane. 'He must be hating this, being scared of small spaces.' If he still was—how could she be sure of anything that had happened in the simulation anymore? What if the Zane she'd known there wasn't real at all, but a virtual version of him? What if this soldier was his true self, and always had been? He might never have changed from the moment they met on Daintree Street...

Finally, they burst into a small cave with numerous exits and Beth desperately scanned the walls, searching for the 'e' sign.

'Well?' Zane demanded as another screech sounded close behind them.

'Look for the 'e'!' said Beth and she quickly explained.

'Found it!' shouted someone and they all turned to race down that tunnel.

The ground became rougher, with large black boulders and sudden gaping sinkholes hampering their way. Dark passages veered off to their left and right, and some had strange white webbing strung across them. There was no time to investigate. The approaching high-pitched hum drove them on.

'Careful!' the captain commanded as their torches flashed around.

The ground sloped steadily upwards, leaving them all puffed and sweating. Then suddenly they burst into an enormous rock-filled cavern and froze, deafened as their helmets crackled with all the reconnecting comms.

'Help! Oh help us!' cried twelve figures stuck to the cavern's wall, trapped by sparkling white webbing. 'Help us!' they begged, waving their arms and legs about.

Everyone rushed over and began tugging at the webbing holding them, but it was hard like shiny crystal strands and wouldn't budge. Beth banged on it with her torch, but it wouldn't shatter either.

'Stand back,' yelled Zane, aiming his rifle at some of the webbing.

'Stop!' the captain shouted, pushing Zane's gun back down. 'You'll kill them!'

Beth felt her heart squeeze. The Zane she knew was truly lost.

But then he stared at the rifle as if seeing it for the first time, shook his head and dropped it like a burning stick.

'Help us! Help!' the web victims cried again.

Whatever was going on with Zane would have to wait—Beth had to free these people before the worm-thing arrived. What could she do? She tried to think quickly. She'd solved the puzzle but where had it led them—into this strange cavern decorated with people, with only torches and guns to save them? Wait, no, that wasn't all—she also had the green stone. She whipped it out of her pouch and gazed at it. Could it be the key?

'You brought the stone?' yelled the captain, noticing. 'The *crystal* stone?'

Zane took a swipe at it, caught one side and pulled.

'Hey!' Beth yelled, clutching it tight.

Zane held fast too and in an instant they were having a stone tug-o-war, just like they had with Kira's bow—and just like with Kira's bow, the black crystal casing cracked open, casting a green glow around the cavern's walls. The stone's blinding light shot up and over the dark rocky surfaces, lighting up thousands of green markings. It was like turning on a light show.

'Oh!' Beth murmured, her eyes wide. The light was dissolving the webbing like melting snow. She eased the stone completely out of its casing and held it up so its strong beams dissolved every piece of web binding the victims to the wall.

They fell to the ground in relief as the green glow fanned out toward the surrounding passages, though it didn't stop the giant worm. Its wailing cry sounded even louder as it sped into the cavern. Everything trembled.

'Watch out!' said Zane, still holding the black crystal casing.

Beth stared at the green stone in her hands, now throbbing as though alive.

'Here it comes!' cried the captain, pushing everyone back. 'Head for that big pile of rocks in the middle!'

Beth and the others ran for what looked like a pyramid of rocks in the cavern's centre. Zane tucked the crystal casing under his arm, grabbed a rock from the floor and threw it at the pulsing worm rushing from the tunnel towards them. Just like the rifle bullets, the rock did nothing except tinkle down its side.

'It's invincible!' Zane cried as he retreated to the pyramid too.

'Get up,' Captain Lang called, helping others climb. 'Get higher!'

Beth scanned the cavern as she climbed one-handed. The ceiling soared so high into the darkness she couldn't see its end. Still she climbed as far as she could, away from the worm below.

It rose up and up, trying to reach them. When it couldn't, it let out a mighty shriek.

'Does it have any vulnerabilities?' the captain asked one of the rescued party. 'Did it attempt to harm any of you?'

'No,' someone replied. 'Just kept us alive.'

Beth steadied herself against the pyramid. If the worm didn't want them for food, what was it after?

Whatever it wanted, it must be something one of them had, because the worm was circling them, humming and squealing with increasingly piercing screeches.

They were cornered.

Chapter 22

Beth studied the worm as it circled them. It had no eyes, no mouth, only a pointy part at the front of its body. A green glow played across its body, and a humming vibrated from all over it. How could they stop it?

Beth bit her lip. Stop it from doing what, though? It hadn't actually hurt anyone…

She glanced at Zane and noticed him staring at the relatively flat top of the pyramid. Had he found another weapon? When he saw her watching him, he pointed at the green stone still clutched in her hand, then at the pyramid's top, which had a pillar with a perfect hollow carved into it—a circular hollow, the exact size and shape of her stone.

'I'll save you all!' Captain Lang suddenly shouted, jumping off the pyramid with a long shard in his hand. He rushed at the worm.

The beast hummed louder and louder until its whole body roared with a frenzy of sound, making the captain sink to his knees and cover his ears with his hands. The worm raised its monstrous body high above the captain, ready to squash him.

'No!' Zane yelled, dropping the crystal casing to jump down and race over to help the captain.

Beth quickly climbed to the pyramid's top pillar, watching as Zane took a flying leap to knock the captain away. The worm shrieked with a pitch so piercing it flooded her helmet but she still managed to slam the green stone into the pillar's hollow.

BOOM!

A sonic thud burst out over the entire cavern, pushing her and everyone else backward. Walls rippled while a rainbow of coloured lights trickled down the sides of the pyramid, seeping like lava down to the worm, which began to flatten itself against the floor.

Zane dragged a stunned Captain Lang back to the pyramid, giving Beth a familiar-looking smile. Was that the old him? Was he back?

The worm lengthened and stretched to form a flat circle around the pyramid, colours seeping over its body, spiralling as though in a dance. Shapes flickered then came into focus as the worm stilled. Like an immense screen, images emerged, deepened and glowed until the cavern floor was filled with visions of travelling through vast and distant galaxies, past moons, planets and suns—a retelling of the cocoon's lengthy journey through space.

Beth marvelled at the epic extent of this creature's travels. Was this what the alien life-form wanted viewers to feel—marvel? She looked down at the glowing stone still under her hand.

Yes, yes it did. It had come here with a message, not of hate or destruction, but of wonder.

'We have sent,' she spoke aloud, although it was not her speaking, but the trilling voice of the cocoon's creators, 'probes such as this one across the universe to find beings such as yourselves—intelligent life-forms capable of empathy for our pet.'

Zane climbed back up beside her and touched her hand. 'We wish to offer transport in stasis,' he said, continuing the message for her, 'to whoever opens this message and contacts us, as a chance to begin a new relationship between our peoples. If you are hearing this, you may choose two ambassadors to send on a journey unlike any your species has ever known. For those you select, the journey will be but a blink though the time more worthwhile than you can imagine.'

This time Beth spoke. 'Your chosen ambassadors would expand their minds as they visit a new world with new technologies. They will explore space on a completely different plane to what may be familiar. Therefore, they must be truly worthy. Choose wisely.'

A magnificent vision of a crystalline alien world beamed over the cavern, showing sparkling towers of glassy-white reaching up to twin suns. And there, deep within the cubical structures, pockets of bushy green—trees!

'Think what we could learn!' Captain Lang said in

awe. 'Whoever went would be famous!'

Beth shivered as the message finished. Everyone was staring at her and Zane and their hands were still touching. She blushed and looked away.

'Perhaps,' suggested the captain, climbing up the pyramid to stand beside them, 'the ones who saved us should be the ones to go? These two have shown compassion, intelligence and the team-effort required for such a mission.' He gestured at Beth and Zane.

Beth stared at the captain, then back at the beautiful pictures splashing over the cavern, so mesmerising. Imagine travelling far across the galaxy, past planets and stars, discovering so many impossible things. She knew Zane would want to in an instant. Together they could do so much for humanity! They would be famous and rich! It was certainly tempting. What did she really have waiting for her back home?

Choose wisely, the message had said of the ambassadors to be selected, *they must be truly worthy.*

She was worthy, wasn't she? She had helped free everyone from the web by dissolving it. She had gotten the green stone into that hollow. She had passed all the tests they'd thrown at her during the simulations. And she couldn't have done any of it without Zane. He was certainly worthy too.

'So, Beth and Zane, do you agree to be our ambassadors?' said Captain Lang.

Zane shifted his weight from one foot to the other and shoved his hands in his pockets. He looked at Beth, a frown where she expected a smile to be. 'I'm sorry, but I can't go,' he glanced down. 'After today, I realise I need to return home. Dad and I have lots of talking to do. He made me do some things I hated, at survival camp and sailing, but I get it now. He was only trying to do what was best for me.' He looked up. 'You understand, don't you, Beth? You've been ready to go home since, like, forever.'

Beth hesitated, staring at the images. 'I don't know anymore.'

'Why?' Zane asked.

'It's just, I've got the chance here to do something really worthwhile with my life. What have I got at home? No friends. Everyone thinks my dad's a loser, and me because of it. At least here I've finally won some respect. These people all think I'm amazing. Whereas back home you'd probably start ignoring me again, like you did when I docked here earlier.'

Zane shook his head. 'That wasn't me. It was weird. I remember not quite making it into a coffin, or did I in the end?' He shook his head again as though to clear his thoughts. 'Then I woke up and forgot all that somehow. I was Corporal Ed with a whole life story. It's hard to explain.' He smiled at her. 'But all the time I thought you were amazing, even before you saved the world, in fact way back when you won the Chameleon Chart. Jumping into the chasm like you did was a bold move. I don't know if I would have dared. I admired that.'

'You had a funny way of showing it.'

'I was jealous! I'm not anymore. We're friends now, remember? After everything we've been through, no one will ever take that away from us. And if anyone back home has a problem with that, well, who cares what they think anyway?'

Beth smiled, relieved and proud at the same time. She had a friend. A real friend. Even winning The Chameleon Chart didn't feel as good as that. She nodded slowly. 'You know, we're not really 'the best of the best' anyway, are we? I left you behind with those zombies…'

'…virus-victims…'

'…whatever they were. Then I stole the stone and kept it hidden. And you know what else? I just don't feel… grown up enough! Surely they have adults they'd rather send? Representing the world—that's really big. Let's go home as heroes. Leave the interstellar travel to someone else.'

'So home then? You sure?'

She nodded firmly.

Zane turned to Captain Lang. 'Thank you, sir, but we're going to say 'no' to your amazing offer. We're ready to go home. Perhaps *you* should go? After all, you showed great bravery facing that worm.'

The captain paused as though deep in thought. Then he suddenly turned to the worm. 'I always did like the idea of spinning across the galaxies.' He gazed at the flashing images. 'Perhaps I'll even find a wife on one of those stars out there.' He spoke into his comms unit. 'Neptune Base Station, we're ready to depart the cocoon. No need for caution. It's safe here now. Send shuttles and please contact ground control. Now,' he addressed those in the cavern, 'anyone know the way out?'

Beth gazed beyond the worm's hard and slippery

surface and noticed a small tunnel with a glowing green 'e' symbol displayed above it, almost like an exit sign, oddly human. She looked down, shuffling her feet. 'Um, I think I see the way out over there,' she pointed.

'Thank you,' said the captain, holding his hand out to shake, 'gamers.'

Beth shook his hand then climbed down the pyramid, heading for the exit. 'Bon voyage.'

'Good luck,' Zane said, following her, along with a number of others.

With a last glance back, Beth saw the captain with his hands over the green stone as if trying it out for size, then she turned to take the glowing 'e' trail all the way to where her shuttle had docked. 'Where did your shuttle dock?' she asked Zane.

'I don't remember.' He sounded sad.

'Wishing you'd gone?'

'Nah, that journey's too far for me. I love space, but it can wait.' He paused. 'Sorry I hit you with that rifle. I kind of lost it back there.'

'Just one more bruise for my collection.' Beth shoved him with her elbow, though doing so hurt her foot. 'Ouch.'

'Still sore?'

She nodded and he slowed to match her speed, walking in silence until they neared the shuttle door. It was black, Beth realised, so perhaps their shuttle had never left them—it had just looked like it had at the time.

Zane sighed as the door slid automatically open.

'What?' Beth asked.

'Well it's going to be tough now since we both really want to get home, yet we've got weeks of sleeping in stasis ahead of us.'

Beth sighed too. 'At least we'll be asleep and won't know it.'

'As long as we don't have such crazy dreams again!'

'Definitely! Though 'the gamers who saved the world' sounds like a good enough dream!' Beth laughed, although the words made her feel uneasy. Wasn't saving the world every gamer's fantasy?

'Do you think they'll reward us?' Zane wondered aloud, strapping himself into a recliner, 'you know, since we saved the—entire—planet?'

Beth nodded slowly. Maybe.

You're the best of the best, the captain had said.

Surely there were better gamers, with more experience...

'Have you ever thought,' she asked Zane, climbing into her seat's safety harness, 'why the cocoon requested kids and not adults?'

Zane shook his head, then shrugged. 'Younger, faster, stronger? Not so set in our ways?'

'Are we though?' Beth clicked her straps into place and that sent a blinding flash around the room.

When she opened her eyes next, nothing was as she'd expected.

Again.

Chapter 23

⌒

Beth squinted against the glare. Was that daylight? Was she home? A breeze tickled the back of her neck. She reached down, feeling soft grass beneath her hands. Yes, she was sitting on grass. But it wasn't home, again. Was it a simulation or another world? Towering tree trunks surrounded her, blue sky peeking through their leafy canopy. Smoke wafted towards her along with the sound of angry roaring beasts. Was she back in the Witheng forest? Was she dreaming while in stasis on a space shuttle home?

'What's going on?'

Turning around, she half expected to see a mutt crouching nearby ready to attack. Instead the grass clearing ended at a chasm as deep as a skyscraper. A tree sloped off its edge and, suspended by his wrists, unconscious over the emptiness, was Zane—a real life hanging man. The bark of the old tree groaned as he swung.

'Zane!' she yelled, her throat so tight it came out as a squeak.

He didn't answer.

She dashed to the edge of the chasm. She had to get him down, but how? There wasn't anything sharp around—not a sharp rock, Witheng spear, Jingum sword or even a pair of scissors…nothing.

The breeze twisted Zane around. Fresh blood stained his top. The slash he'd got from the Hupuleq was back, dripping slowly. The gash on his neck from the rockfall glistened too.

'You want to rescue him?' came a slithery voice.

Beth froze.

Striding from the trees was a tall figure with dark hair, a moustache and bright green eyes. He was dressed in a cape—exactly like Tordon's gamemaster, the Chameleon, who ushered winners into the Golden House of Fame.

'You're…'

'Yes.' He beamed, spreading his arms wide while stalking closer, his green eyes almost luminous against his skin. 'Do you like my home?' He gestured at the forest around them.

Beth remembered DaveT had seen Kaleski among the trees of the Witheng forest. Did he mean this guy? She supposed Kaleski might have made the Chameleon look like his own appearance. 'Wait, are you Kaleski or the Chameleon?'

'Which do you think?'

Beth stared into his green eyes—hadn't she seen them before, in some of the other worlds, in other creatures as well? 'I don't know,' she said, cautious. 'I've never met Kaleski, though DaveT said he came through here.'

'I have done, from time to time. What do you think?'

'Um…'

'Lost for words?' The Chameleon swung back his jacket to reveal two steel Kumdo swords at his hip. He rested his hands on their hilts. 'I understand you're this year's winner?'

Beth nodded, not taking her eyes off the swords.

'Great game this year, don't you think?'

'A bit more involved than I would have liked.'

He shrugged. 'Winning comes with its own challenges.'

'Did I even really win? Was I supposed to jump off that chasm or not?'

'You tell me.' He gestured at Zane. 'Would you do it in real life?'

Beth shifted her weight off her sore foot. Could she even climb that tree right now? 'Anyway,' she remembered, 'this isn't real life. I'm back in a simulation.'

'If you want to take that chance,' he looked at her foot. 'Was your foot always sore?'

'No, a snake bit it.'

'And has the pain gone away, as it would in a simulation?'

Beth paused to think. No, it had hurt in that virus-victim hospital, and in the Neptune cocoon, which meant…what? Had the gateways all been real after all, including the cocoon? It could have been a different dimension of Earth. The captain had never said what the simulated tests had involved. It could have been standard survival camp stuff for all she knew.

'I'll tell you what,' the Chameleon said, his smile

turning oily, 'defeat me and you can have your friend back. After all, life is just a game, don't you think?'

There was a flash of steel and a thump at her feet. Embedded in the ground was a sword.

Beth quickly picked it up. It was much lighter than any tribesman's and she could swing it with some control.

'That's the way,' the Chameleon said with a terrifying smile, gripping his own sword in both hands. 'You know, anyone else would have accepted the honour of travelling the universe as Earth's representatives. Why didn't you? You could have gone home *after* travelling the universe.'

'I wasn't worthy of the honour.'

'Let's find out. Prepare,' he said, slowly moving towards her. Then, without warning, he lunged.

Beth blocked him, then stepped back.

They circled each other, then Beth charged. The Chameleon blocked her so hard she almost lost her grip altogether. Coming at an angle this time, he tried to prick her side, but she ducked out the way. He edged closer and their swords tapped a few times, testing. From watching VODs of Kumdo battles, Beth knew real sword fights could be over in seconds. All it took was one slash across a hand or a strike on an arm, and she mightn't be able to hold her sword at all. So she didn't dare raise her sword too high, lest he lunged underneath. She concentrated on anticipating his next move instead.

'Come on, Bethlyn,' the Chameleon teased. 'Why are you waiting?'

'Where's the gateway back home, is it in one of these trees?'

'Defeat me and I'll tell you.'

Tightening her grip, she lunged at his left shoulder.

He blocked, winking at her as they both recovered. 'I thought you were a winner. You aren't even trying. Maybe you're just playing after all, a loser.'

Her face flushed as his words struck home. 'I am not a loser,' she growled. 'I won!'

'Some champion you are,' the Chameleon's face twisted into a sneer, 'can't even beat an old man like me.'

'Less talking, more action,' she snarled, trying to spike his left shoulder again.

'Is that all you want, my shoulder?' He lowered his sword and leant forward. 'Go on then, take it. Slice it if you want, jab it, whatever, I don't care—just get this party started.'

Beth held her sword steady, although her arms were tiring.

'Coward,' the Chameleon jeered at her, his face reddening. 'You're a disgrace to my game. Where's all your fight?'

'I don't see much fight coming from you either,' she spat back.

'Beth?' A weak voice floated over the chasm. Zane was waking up. 'Oh no—Beth, where are you? Get me down! Help! I am *not* dangling above a chasm,' he chanted. 'I am *not*...nope. Beth!' He twisted his legs to face the clearing. 'You've got to be kidding,' he said when he saw who she was fighting. 'Run!' he yelled at her. 'Get away!'

'No!' she shouted. 'I won't leave you again!'

Swinging wildly with her sword, she ran at the

Chameleon. Her attack took the Chameleon by surprise and she got him—just a short slice on his upper arm, but it was something.

'Very good,' he congratulated her. 'What else have you got?'

Roaring like a Witheng tribesman, she ran at him again, swiping with all her might. He blocked her and his sword went flying, disappearing into the bushes.

'Go Beth!' Zane yelled in excitement.

The Chameleon smirked. 'You have to kill me to defeat me.'

'What? You don't have a sword. I've won. Now let Zane down and show us the gateway.'

'You think being without a weapon will stop me overpowering you?' He stepped closer. 'I could easily take your sword with my bare hands. You are no match for me. So strike me down now or you *and* your friend will die.'

Beth shook her head, confused. *Would* they die? Was this real life or a simulation? Surely it was a simulation?

'Let me guess, you're thinking that you can't die in a simulation, right? Ah but you can,' the Chameleon tapped his head, 'you can die in here. It's not all bad, losing your mind. Think about Kira—she seemed happy, right? DaveT and Jumbie. What is waiting for you anyway, back home? You think people will simply like you now you're a winner?' he taunted. 'At least here you might grow to *think* you had real friends.'

Beth growled. She had real friends—she had Zane.

He *was* real. Wasn't he?

Either way, if there was one thing she'd learnt more

than anything since entering that house on Daintree Street, it was that killing was never the answer—even if people said it was. If she struck the Chameleon down now, without him having a weapon, it wouldn't be self-defence anymore—it would be an execution.

She waved her sword at him, hoping to drive him back.

He simply stood his ground. 'Do it,' he hissed, his hands by his side.

'Do you want to die,' she tapped her head, 'in here?'

'You want to go home, don't you? I'm only trying to help. This is the way.'

Beth bit her lip, then stared at the Chameleon and let the tip of her sword drop to the ground. 'No, killing you is *not* the answer.'

'Yes, it is!' His eyes flared with anger.

'All I want is my friend back and to go home.' She stepped around him, closer to the tree. 'I don't want to kill you. I'm not going to kill you.'

'You have to!' Flecks of spit shot from his mouth and stuck to his moustache. 'That's what winners do, they kill their enemies!'

Beth nodded at the bushes where his sword had disappeared. 'Then make me!'

'Argh!' he grunted, stomping off toward the trees.

Once he was rummaging through leaves, Beth quickly hobbled across the clearing to the sloping tree. She jabbed her sword into the bark as high as she could, then clawed her way up the trunk until she was within reaching distance of Zane's ropes. Once steady, gripping onto the trunk with her legs, she reached down, grabbed her sword, then paused. What was she thinking? If she cut Zane's ropes, he would fall!

'Beth?' Zane interrupted her thoughts, his eyes staring into hers. 'One of the best gamers I know taught me that a real warrior sometimes has to take chances to win, remember?'

'What?'

'Cut me down.'

'But you'll fall.'

Zane pointed his foot at the base of the tree. 'See those roots sticking out?'

Beth examined the twisted roots jutting over the chasm searching for earth. She nodded.

'Once you cut me, I'll fall directly on top of those and grab on.'

'No way, you'll miss!'

'Don't you trust me by now?'

Beth searched the chasm and the tree for another solution. 'There has to be an alternative.'

'Just cut below that knot so my hands are free when I fall.' He began swinging. 'Ready? One, two...'

'Wait! There has to be a...'

'Aha!' yelled the Chameleon, brandishing his sword. 'Found it.'

'Quick, Beth,' Zane yelled as the Chameleon sprinted to the tree. 'We can overpower him together!'

Beth took a deep breath, braced herself against the trunk, then angled her sword and sawed under the rope's knot just as the Chameleon began to climb.

His weight bounced the tree just as she cut through the rope's last strand.

Zane's hands parted, but with the Chameleon's extra weight, the trunk bent too far out for Zane to reach the tree roots below.

He fell with only air below him.

'Zane!' Beth screamed, reaching for his hands. Only, with the vibrations from the Chameleon's climb, she lost her grip on the tree.

'No!' cried the Chameleon.

She plummeted into the chasm after Zane, screaming as she fell.

Chapter 24

Beth's screams turned into shrieks as the chasm's sides rushed past. Zane was just below, falling and screaming too as the ground rushed up fast to meet them. This was it—the end of everything—and yet...it was the most unreal experience of her life.

She stopped screaming.

This *couldn't* be happening. Who had duels with swords at the edge of chasms? Who tied people to trees then taunted others into killing them? Something hadn't felt right to Beth as they were leaving the Neptune cocoon, and now she felt it again. It simply wouldn't happen. Why would a gamemaster want to kill her and Zane anyway?

Life is just a game, the Chameleon had said.

And so was this. It had to be. 'No more games, Bethlyn!' she screamed.

She glanced up at the shrinking sky. The sun even beamed a little brighter just for her. Then it flashed and she slammed into hard ground.

Only it wasn't a massive slam, more like a thud, as if

she'd only tripped over, and as the sun's flash faded, she wasn't at the base of any chasm, but in a small windowless room in a house, lit by heated glass tanks.

Beth's eyes adjusted in the dim light. A steady hum filled her ears—the hum of tiny filters in the tanks—and an odd whispering sound.

'What's that noise?' Zane asked, sitting up and rubbing his eyes.

'Zane!' She nudged his arm, gleefully. 'You're okay!'

'I *am* okay,' he said, looking amazed.

Beth was so glad to have him back she couldn't stop smiling.

'Hey,' he said, looking around, 'I think we're actually home this time.'

Beth looked too. Wooden floorboards. Flaky floral wallpaper covered three walls with a thin white coat of paint. Was this really, finally, Kaleski's house on Daintree Street?

Zane pulled up his top and checked his chest. There wasn't a scratch on him. He checked his neck and wrists. No lights, no sheer webbing coating his hands, just plain white wristbands, like a memento of a bad dream.

Beth's hands and wrists were the same—no webbing, only the bands. She stood up and tested her foot. It felt fine. 'So it was simulations all along?' she murmured. 'The luminous virus-victims, the giant fish, the Neptune Space Station—everything?'

Zane nodded as if realising it for the first time. 'Must have been one virtual world after another, ever since we went through that Black-Door-With-No-Doorknob. So I never dangled you over a pit of snakes using only tree roots, or fired an arrow into a sun?'

Beth crouched beside him. 'I guess not.'

'Wow,' Zane looked down at his chest, 'that was one really, really good simulation. I was slashed by a monster, bleeding and everything! And on that tree just now, I really thought I was going to die!'

'Me too.'

For a moment they were silent, Zane slowly straightening his top.

'It's actually not a very nice feeling,' he said eventually. 'It feels like I've been cheated of something.'

Beth nodded. 'We never agreed to it.'

'And what *is* that noise?'

The whispering was getting louder.

As Beth moved to get a closer look at the tanks, she noticed a damp musky smell, just like the cave. Her nose wrinkled, then she sucked in her breath. The tanks were full of writhing snakes. She backed away, not taking her eyes off the creatures. Dozens of scaly heads turned her way, their beady eyes following her every move. Beth jumped as something clammy touched her fingers, but it was just Zane's hand.

'I hate snakes,' he moaned. 'Hey, can you hear that?'

'What?'

'Exactly. Nothing.'

Beth found herself holding her breath. Zane was right, apart from the humming and hissing from the snake tanks, there were no sounds at all. 'Time to leave,' she said, scanning the walls. 'Where's the door?'

'Um,' Zane looked around as well, 'there?'

Behind the snake tanks was a glass partition dividing their room from another dark one. A slim glass door stood closed in the corner. Beth edged around the snake tanks and Zane followed, screwing up his face in distaste.

'Is anybody there?' Beth yelled through the glass, her heart pounding as she tugged on the door handle. It was locked. Her chest felt tight.

Then, a faint clunk.

'Who's there?'

Silence.

Strange lights flickered, then multiple transparent figures began to move through the glass wall towards them—tribesmen, mutts, luminous virus-victims, snakes and mammoth fish, even Captain Lang, all mumbling to themselves or snapping at something.

'Watch out,' Beth hissed, pulling Zane out of the way of a desert warrior—except Zane didn't move fast enough and the warrior walked straight through him. Where were all these figures coming from and why were they still seeing them? Beth cupped her hands between her eyes and the glass. It was hard to see, but there seemed to be a large metallic table on the other side, with eleven creatures hunched around it.

Each creature held a small box with strange bulbs on the edges. When a light glowed in the middle of the table, they looked directly up at Beth and Zane, then frantically began tapping at the bulbs. Their eyes were black and twice the size of a normal person's. Their skin was smooth and ghostly pale.

'What are they?' she whispered to Zane, pointing.

Zane cupped his own hands against the glass. 'I don't know. But look at their hands.'

Beth narrowed her eyes. The creatures' hands were coated with the same sheer webbing that used to be on her and Zane's hands, and the boxes were physically stuck to the creatures' white wristbands.

'And what is that smell?' Zane said, grimacing. 'It's like when you overcharge your game console with the wrong plug and fry it.'

'Like electric trains.' Beth nodded. Now they were away from the snakes, the smell was getting stronger too, as if something electrical was smouldering nearby. Beth glanced down. Puffs of smoke were spiralling up from the bands around their wrists. 'Quick,' she yelled, 'we've got to get them off!' This time when she tugged, the band stretched like rubber, although still too small to slip over her hand. Whereas the mesh she thought had gone became visible again, shrivelling and lifting from all over her body. She could feel it on her face, arms, chest—everywhere! She ripped at it and nudged Zane. 'Look, it's coming off!'

'Finally.' Zane tugged at the fibres over his own body. 'I thought it was just on our hands, it's everywhere! No wonder we felt everything—all the fibres criss-crossing over our bodies. Imagine the technology involved! It was practically invisible most of the time!'

With each piece they removed, more transparent images around them faded.

Poof!

A flash made them freeze. Then more smoke. The glass wall behind the snake tanks was disappearing, flickering until it didn't exist anymore, and instead of eleven creatures there were now eleven kids sitting around a conference table staring at normal computer screens, each of them wearing simple white bands around their wrists. On the far wall hung two Jingum swords. Under those, another snake tank hummed.

Crackle!

Flash!

Then everything was still and silent again.

Beth and Zane finished pulling off their webbing, though the white bands were still too tight to pull over their wrists.

'Who are they?' Zane said, tugging at his bands as he crept through the smoke closer to the kids sitting around the table.

They were all tapping at keyboards and randomly touching the dual screens before them, completely ignoring Beth and Zane. One screen showed the market place of Sheikh Zidan, another showed the grass play area with the hanging swings, while the twinned screen of each showed lines of code. Further along was a monitor for the rice paddy. Another showed the Neptune cocoon.

'This is real time now, right?' Beth whispered, studying a monitor and watching luminous virus-victims fighting over what looked like brains.

Into Tordon

Zane pointed at a guy sitting on the far side of the table. 'Isn't that Jumbie with the scar from the desert?'

'Yes!'

'DaveT!' Zane yelled at one of the boys, waving a hand in front of his face. But he didn't even look up from his screen.

Beth moved behind DaveT's chair and studied the forest scene. The screen next to it was filled with lines of code and more was appearing as DaveT's fingers moved without a break. In the top left corner of each screen was the name of his Tordon character, 'DaveT'. 'He's recreating the forest for the game of Tordon,' she guessed.

'So what's the point of it all?' Zane snapped.

Chair legs scraped across floorboards as a boy got up and moved to the far end of the room, where a control panel was mounted onto the wall. Underneath it was a long narrow refreshments table full of drinks and snacks. While the boy helped himself, Beth hurried over to jump in front of him, waving her hands and yelling. He didn't respond.

'They can't hear us,' Beth said, standing still again to listen to the snake tanks humming. 'Wait, what's that?' The snake tanks *weren't* the only noise. From the other end of the table, someone was muttering and whimpering.

Zane looked up. Then he grabbed Beth's arm and pointed to an old man crouched beside a young girl that looked very familiar.

'Kira?'

Beth and Zane edged closer.

The old man looked familiar too, though there was

an urgency in his voice that seemed too private to listen to, as well as tears in his eyes. 'Did it work?' he said to the girl. 'Did it make a difference? Can you hear me? Say something Kira, please. I'll try harder, I promise.'

Zane raised his eyebrows at Beth.

A floorboard under Beth creaked and the old man looked up, his sad eyes hardening. He clenched his fists. 'It's all your fault!' he snapped. 'Now I have to fix all that you've broken.'

'Fix what?' Zane asked. 'Who are you?'

The old man stood. 'You're just like the others—a disgrace to my game. Some winner!' he sneered at Beth.

Beth stepped closer. 'Hey, I recognise your voice. You still do your own voiceovers, don't you? I hear your voice on the game all the time. Zane, this is Aaron Kaleski, creator and developer of Tordon.'

'Mr Kaleski?' Zane asked. 'I thought you moved to India?'

'Ha! I would have if Ripple hadn't fired me.'

'So they *did* fire you!' Beth glanced at Zane.

'It wasn't my fault.'

'*What* wasn't your fault?' Zane asked quietly.

'She,' Kaleski pointed at Beth, 'she was supposed to win the final level by killing the Chameleon. If she'd done what she was supposed to, I would have found it.'

'Found what?'

'The bug! The virus! Why else do you think they're like this?' Kaleski shuffled down the room. 'They've gone mad, poor kids. Once they're in they won't come out— they don't even know they should! Now they're stuck in there for another month, until I can find a real winner. It's the only thing that hasn't happened yet. Someone has to win.' He paced further. 'I should have focussed on inventing another game, get more players in quicker. Now we all have to wait again.'

'How long have they been stuck here?' Beth looked from one screen to the next, recognising one gamer's character name after another. They were all past winners of The Chameleon Chart. 'I haven't seen some of these players online in months. Is this where they've all been? You've been holding them captive?'

'Not me,' he snapped, 'the game.'

'Why don't you just turn it off?' demanded Beth.

'Don't you think I would if I could?' Kaleski glanced back at Kira. 'See these?' He held up his hands. Two red bands were fastened around his wrists. 'If I pull the plug while these are still on we could all go insane. That's what happened with the original testers. I won't risk doing that to my daughter.'

'So that's why you got fired,' said Zane.

'Kira was helping me. She was so good at games. I thought I'd fixed it too. Stupid, so stupid. I never should have let her play.'

'Um...Beth,' Zane warned, putting his hand on her arm while looking straight at Kaleski.

Strange shadows were flashing across the man's face. It was almost as if two people were occupying the same space.

'You,' Kaleski turned and snapped at Beth, 'you were supposed to win. Everyone else lost, all of them, all of them. So I still can't find it. Where is it? Where is it?' He shuffled back down the room again and picked up a screwdriver from the table. 'I've got to find it. Then I'll show them. They'll buy my game and we'll be rich, Kira. Just hold on. I'll get you out.' The lights started to flicker. 'What's wrong now?' He grunted at a bright flash and started shuffling towards them.

Beth blinked, and for a split second Kaleski looked like the Chameleon, creeping towards them grinning and wielding a knife. 'Zane?'

The same light flashed again, sparking as if something was short-circuiting, and the old man was Kaleski again, holding a screwdriver.

There was the smell of smoke again, and another flash.

'Come here, you,' snarled the Chameleon this time, towering over them.

'Zane,' Beth whispered, backing around the table. 'Why are we still seeing this when we ripped off our web-interface?' She glanced at the kids hunched over the table. Parts of them looked like pale creatures with boxes, other parts looked like normal kids typing on keyboards. The Chameleon's face flashed with Kaleski's then back again. The different images were flashing on and off like a strobe.

'The bands!' cried Zane, tugging on his. 'We're still getting something through our wristbands!'

'You play to win,' Kaleski spat, creeping closer.

'You're insane,' Zane said, moving in front of Beth. 'Stay back.'

'Why didn't you win?' Kaleski brandished his

screwdriver. 'I could have found it. She would've been free.'

'You don't know that,' Zane yelled. 'You said it yourself—you don't know what the bug is. How many more 'testers' will you let play the game? How many more will you trap in here, just so you can find it? The police will find you soon. What about all these kids' families? They must be so worried! Don't you care about them?'

'Wait,' Beth cried, staring at Zane. 'Why aren't we trapped? We didn't win the game, but we're not trapped like the others.' She gestured at the other gamers.

Kaleski stopped moving and stared at the ground in thought. 'You should have been trapped. The game is only programmed for winners or losers. You must defeat the Chameleon to win. If he defeats you, you lose. Until now, all the losers end up trapped, lost in the worlds. But not you.'

'Because we didn't win or lose. The Chameleon didn't defeat us. We fell.'

Kaleski gazed around the room, hazy from wisps of smoke, flickering as lights flashed. 'You've broken it.'

Seeing his opportunity Zane leapt forward, grabbing the old man's arm and trying to knock the screwdriver from his grasp, the knife from the Chameleon.

Kaleski gripped harder and they struggled against the table, jostling the gamers. Zane just squeezed tighter and tighter until, with a final flick, the screwdriver flew across the room, stabbing the control panel over the refreshments table. Sparks flew out like a firework.

'No!' Kaleski screamed, shuffling over to the panel.

There was a blinding flash, then the entire room was plunged into darkness.

Beth felt a strange buzzing in her head, then a burning on her wrists. Smoke was coming from her wristbands. The heat was unbearable. Tiny cracks in the rubber were spreading like webs. Beth gritted her teeth against the burning and pulled with all her strength.

Snap!

The band fell into her hand. She could hear Zane grunting.

'Zane, keep pulling. They come off!'

She did the same with her other wrist and heard snaps as Zane tore his free too.

A moment later, emergency lights came on, bathing the room in a pale yellow light.

Beth blinked, then squinted through the haze to see what had happened. She gasped. 'Zane, look.' She pointed at the table, her hand shaking. 'The kids.'

Before their eyes, the gamers were fading, dissolving, one by one, just as the other characters had done earlier in the tank room. The gamers weren't real.

No, Beth realised, not all the gamers. One figure remained solid and she was staring around her in confusion as she tore at her own bands. A moment later they were in pieces on the table.

Kaleski stumbled over to his daughter. 'Kira?' he murmured, wrapping his arms around her. 'Oh Kira.'

'Dad? Oh Dad, it is you!' She threw her arms around him.

'I'm sorry, I'm so sorry. It's over,' he murmured into

her hair. 'Thank you, Beth, Zane. You brought her back to me. Thank you.'

Zane exhaled slowly, then smiled at Beth, until a loud click made them both jump. A door had opened at the back of the room and, while it was faint, the unmistakable glow of daylight shone through it.

Beth peered out to see a shadowy wooden staircase. It was Kaleski's hallway.

'Let's go,' Kaleski said, 'quickly. We have to get them all out!'

'All?' Beth said. 'There's only Kira and us.'

'Are you mad?' Kaleski screamed at her. As he gestured around the table, Beth suddenly understood. Two red bands still hung on Kaleski's wrists. They hadn't cracked when the control panel short-circuited.

'He doesn't know,' she gasped. 'Zane, he's still stuck in the simulation. Look!' She pointed as his wrists.

'Quick!' Kaleski demanded, stepping away from Kira. Sweat gleamed on his forehead. His head started twitching from side to side as he clenched his jaw, green eyes flashing. 'Quick! The Chameleon's fighting back! He doesn't want to lose! I can't hold him off, please hurry,' he begged. 'The Chameleon is still here!'

'Mr Kaleski, we need to get your bands off,' Beth begged. 'You didn't trap the other gamers. They *did* get out. Kira is going to be free too. And you! Here, let me help you.'

'No!' He stepped away from all of them. 'You have to leave. Now!'

'Please Dad.' Kira reached for his hand. 'She's telling

the truth. Come with me and I'll help you. You're still in the simulation. There's no one else here. Others did come, I remember now, but when they lost they simply left the house and went home.'

'But, if others came,' Zane asked Kira, 'why haven't we heard about all this in the chatroom?'

'Security systems,' Kira explained. 'They delete unwanted comments from the chatroom automatically. Lock out certain players. Dad, there really isn't anyone else here.'

Kaleski closed his eyes, took a large shuddering breath then looked up at them again, calmer. 'You're right. It just feels so real. Now let's go together, please.' He gestured for Beth to lead the way.

Beth wanted to sprint down the hallway ahead of them all, feel the hazy sun of home on her face. But Kaleski looked so weak, shuffling forward supported by Zane and Kira. They needed to stay together and help each other. So she edged across the dim floor, checking for any obstacles, and savoured the fresh but thick air breezing down the hallway towards them and the distant sound of cars from the street.

As they reached the door, she looked up at the sky. It wasn't as blue as some of those she'd seen lately, but at least she knew this sky well. And there was the driveway. She stepped onto it and blinked. It felt like she and Zane had walked down it a lifetime ago. Wait, was that VlahPaul, Wolk and 6thDan still walking away?

They'd been gone no time at all!

No wonder no one else had spoken about the house on Daintree Street. If Zane and Kira weren't with her now, she'd probably be confused and questioning whether any of it had happened at all. She might even think it had all been a dream.

'Beth!' Zane called out, panic in his voice.

She looked back inside the house.

Kaleski was slumped against a wall just beside the doorway, cowering from something, his face crumpled in shock. 'No!' he groaned. 'They're are back! That's impossible. Get away, get away!'

'What is it, Dad?' asked Kira, still holding his arm.

'The game…it short-circuited. No-one's controlling it now. So why are they here?' His eyes flicked about wildly. 'It must be…it's re-setting itself. Get out! The mutts are coming!'

'Dad, come on!' shouted Kira, tugging on his arm. 'It's just your wristbands.'

Zane went to pull the old man out the door but he pushed them both away.

'It's too late for me!'

'We're going to have to carry him out.' Zane told Beth as she hurried over to help. 'Ready?'

Beth nodded and the three of them heaved him to the doorstep. The daylight grew brighter and brighter, until… flash! A shockwave made them drop Kaleski and they all fell backwards, out onto the driveway.

'Dad?' Kira yelled.

Slumped on the hallway floor, Kaleski ran his

hands over the floorboards. 'The leaves,' he moaned, 'everywhere.'

Kira went to help him up, but hit an invisible barrier. 'Dad?'

He turned his back on them, then slowly stood up and spread his arms wide. Fibres shot out from the door frame, coating his body and limbs. He looked around, amazed as if grass were sprouting around his feet and trees soaring overhead. When he finally looked back at them, a hint of the Chameleon stared out of the old man's eyes. An evil grin crossed his face. 'The game ends now,' he said, and the Black-Door-With-No-Doorknob fell down with a slam, shutting him inside.

'Dad,' Kira sobbed, collapsing on the doorstep. 'He's trapped in there!'

Beth crouched and put an arm around her shoulders. 'He'll find a way out, I know he will. Especially now he doesn't have to worry about you.'

'You don't know that!' Kira cried. 'He's in there all alone!'

'Yes, but he's the best of the best!' Zane said, crouching by her other side. 'He's Aaron Kaleski. If anyone can find a bug in a game, it's him.' He glanced at Beth. 'And, now we know about it, we can organise a rescue from the outside. We'll get all sorts of people onto it, like my dad. He really knows a lot.'

Kira sniffed, but glanced at him with hope.

Beth felt for the girl. She'd only just been reunited with her father. To lose him so soon had to be like a thousand nightmares come true. Beth hugged her and helped her up, then took a deep breath and gazed down the street towards home. Kira wasn't the only one with a father she loved. She glanced at Zane, who nodded.

It was time to go home.

One Year Later

It was the first time Beth had sat at her computer since her time in the house on Daintree Street. Zane, DaveT, Kira and herself had been spending more time at each other's houses rather than playing games online, because if there was one thing Beth had learnt from going into Tordon, it was that there were no shortcuts to making friends.

'Here you go, Bethie,' her dad said, passing her a fizzy drink and a chicken sandwich. 'I'm off to work, so don't play too long, your eyes will go funny.'

'Yes, Dad.'

'Remember I'll be late home too.'

'I know. Someone's going on a date!' she teased. Things had changed a lot over the past year.

'Yeah, yeah,' her dad smiled, closing her bedroom door.

The movement made the newspaper clippings on her wall flutter. Beth was pictured in one of them as the inspiration behind the revolutionary new game being released by Ripple today. It was a 'local girl done good' story. Dad was in the photo alongside her, quoted as saying his daughter's achievements had inspired him to face life afresh too. Beth was so proud of him—a new job, new girlfriend, things were going great.

After Kaleski had been trapped inside the game, he'd done just as Zane had said and worked on the game's problems from the inside, while technicians worked on the outside. Finally, the game was bug-free. Kaleski had been freed, sold his game to Ripple and, in thanks for their help, he'd shared the money with everyone who had ever 'tested' it for him, including Beth and Zane.

Beth went to pull down the sleeves of her top, then realised she didn't have to anymore. She could afford a new top every growth spurt now—more if it took her fancy, which it rarely did. Instead she wiped her sweaty palms on her jeans and typed 'The Chameleon' into her search engine. A familiar-looking house appeared in the centre of the screen. Her heart pounded. This was it, the moment she'd been waiting for all year—the moment she got to face her arch enemy again, this time on her own terms. Ripple's new game allowed gamers to compete in teams, and she wanted more than anything to win the chance of taking part in the game's *virtual* Grand Final with her friends. After all, they'd had enough practice.

Logged in and ready to go, she switched on her motion-sensor interface. She'd wave open the onscreen door as soon as she got a certain notification in the screen's chat list. A few moments later, she got three.

Zane007—Ready to play?

Beth smiled and typed her reply.

BGwarrior—Only because I have the best partner.

Another avatar appeared in the chat list.

DaveT—Partner? Make that a team.
KiraSun—I'm here too!

Beth took a deep breath and smiled to herself. It was time. She gestured at the door and the countdown started.
3—2—1
Let the game begin.

About the Author

Z.F. Kingbolt is a
Northern Beaches Writers' Group pseudonym
Into Tordon is a collaborative project between:

Editor-in-Chief
Zena Shapter

Editors
Zoya Nojin • Zena Shapter

Authors
Leah Boonthanom • Tracey Jackson • Liz Michell •
Mijmark • Tony McFadden • Zoya Nojin •
Kristin Prescott • Zena Shapter • Kirsten Taylor

zfkingbolt.com

Acknowledgements

We would like to thank our wonderful families for their constant support and love. We could not have written this book, or any of our individual writing projects, without your understanding and patience. Thank you.

Thank you, Anna Solding at MidnightSun Publishing, for bringing *Into Tordon* to life. Thank you Lynette Washington for your keen eye. Thank you Mat Wilson and Abigail Nathan for your expert advice on gaming and technology. Thank you Fi Michell for creating with us while you could.

Finally, thank you dear readers for welcoming Z.F. Kingbolt into your lives. We hope this story gives you an adventure you won't forget, and the odd chuckle along the way.

Find us online at zfkingbolt.com

MidnightSun Publishing

We are a small, independent publisher based in Adelaide, South Australia. Since publishing our first novel, Anna Solding's *The Hum of Concrete* in 2012, MidnightSun has gone from strength to strength.

We create books that are beautifully produced, unusual, sexy, funny and poignant. Books that challenge, excite, enrage and overwhelm. When readers tell us they have lost themselves in our stories, we rejoice in a job well done.

MidnightSun Publishing aims to reach new readers every year by consistently publishing excellent books. Welcome to the family!

midnightsunpublishing.com

MidnightSun   *Publishing Brilliance*